# AT THE STROKE OF THIRTY

Rebecca Paulinyi

Copyright © 2022 Rebecca Paulinyi

All rights reserved

This is a work of fiction. Names, characters, businesses, places, events and incidents are either the products of the author's imagination or used in a fictitious manner. Any resemblance to actual persons, living or dead, or actual events is purely coincidental.

No part of this book may be reproduced, or stored in a retrieval system, or transmitted in any form or by any means, electronic, mechanical, photocopying, recording, or otherwise, without express written permission of the publisher.

Cover design by: Dawn Taylor

*This book is dedicated to all the people who were instrumental in helping me immediately after my stroke: my husband Josh, my mum Angela, my sister Katie, and my amazing friends Jenny, Izzy and Kayley.*

# CONTENTS

Title Page
Copyright
Dedication
Chapter One — 1
Chapter Two — 25
Chapter Three — 49
Chapter Four — 70
Chapter Five — 91
Chapter Six — 99
Chapter Seven — 128
Chapter Eight — 141
Chapter Nine — 164
Chapter Ten — 195
Chapter Eleven — 211
Chapter Twelve — 228
Afterword — 235
The Thirties Club — 237

# Books By This Author

# CHAPTER ONE

Macy Maxwell had never been in an ambulance before. But all that was to change on the day before her thirtieth birthday.

All in all, she had been rather well for her whole life. Even when she had been born, her mother had been home within a few hours. And no childhood illness or adult mishap had sent her for an overnight stay at the local hospital.

Not that there hadn't been one or two close calls. At eighteen, drunk on freedom and too much alcohol at university, she had fallen down a flight of stairs and fractured her ankle. But thanks – or not – to the copious amounts of alcohol she had been drinking, she didn't really notice how painful it was until the next day, when she promptly took herself off to A and E, and was home by the evening.

And now, at twenty-nine, nights out drinking were not so frequent – but not as infrequent as she might have expected. Was her life where she had thought it would be at the grand old age of twenty-nine? No, she supposed it was not. If she were honest with herself, she had pictured a good many things being in place in her life on the cusp of turning thirty. Husband; children; good job;

owning her own house… So many things were not a reality.

But she wasn't sad about her life. She did have a good job – well, one she enjoyed and that brought in a decent wage, anyway. And she had fun going out with her friends: cocktail nights, fancy meals, shopping trips. And there had been boyfriends, on and off – but no one she could see herself spending the rest of her life with. She didn't own her own house, but she rented a snazzy flat in the centre of Newcastle, with a balcony that overlooked the river. Many things that felt like success – even if it wasn't the success she had perhaps envisioned.

It certainly wasn't the success her parents had envisioned for her. They still lived in the middle of nowhere in rural Northumberland, and whenever they rang, they asked whether she had found anybody, whether she was considering buying a house, and whether any of her friends had children. The not-so-subtle hints were hard to ignore, and hard not to take personally – but she had to remind herself that the things that she enjoyed in her life would not be things that they had desired for themselves. When an old friend from uni visited, she was in awe of Macy's flat, and the freedom that life in the city with a decent salary afforded her.

So perhaps her life was different than she expected – but different wasn't bad. Her life wasn't bad – in fact, many days, it felt like she had everything worked out.

It wasn't unusual for Macy to spend an evening on the sofa with a bottle of wine and a takeaway, but that night she opted for pasta, tea, and a packet of chocolate biscuits.

She knew she would be drinking on the night of her birthday party – after all, one only turned thirty once – and so a quiet night that Friday night seemed like a good plan. Saturday, too, she thought she would spend quietly – perhaps organising the house, and making sure her outfit was ready for her birthday bash on the Sunday. She had even managed to book Monday off work, to ensure that she did not have to restrain herself in her celebrations, as well as having the Friday off as a birthday treat to herself.

Yes, everything was lined up perfectly, and although thirty had always seemed like a big milestone, she was finding herself more excited than scared about reaching it. It did seem rather grown-up; but then perhaps that's how everyone felt about turning a milestone birthday. Perhaps no-one ever really felt grown-up enough for the age they were. Except teenagers, she thought; they always thought they were more grown-up than they were.

She considered a film, but after flicking through the options available, she settled on binge-watching the latest medical drama that everyone was going on about. She was not particularly fond of needles or blood, but found she could watch these shows without cringing too much. She certainly could never have been a doctor or a nurse: far too squeamish. But it was amazing how several hours binge-watching a medical show could make you feel like you knew all the terminology, and by 11 o'clock, her head was full of terms she would probably never use again, and diagnoses of rare diseases that she ended up looking up on her phone to see whether they were even real.

Her phone buzzed twice during the evening, but other than that she had very little contact with the outside world. That seem to be the way of things, at the minute. Some days were full of social interaction: a day at work, surrounded by people, then an evening in the pub perhaps. Or a night out surrounded by strangers who became friends with the help of alcohol.

And then days like this where she saw no-one, spoke to no-one. She wasn't even sure she heard her own voice today. Perhaps she should get a cat, she thought – and then she remembered that her flat was not suitable for a cat, and she probably wasn't even allowed one anyway. And did talking to a pet really count as conversation? But maybe it would be better than not speaking for the best part of the weekend.

*How was your weekend? Looking forward to seeing*

*you on Sunday for your party! Mum X*

Macy smiled. Mum still felt the need to sign off her texts, even after years of having a phone and knowing that her name came up when the message arrived. She was looking forward to seeing her parents, for it had been a while since she had last seen them. Somehow the distance between them, although not that great, seemed too much to travel for a weekend. Although it would mean a little more conversation…

She wondered how Mum and Dad would cope with her friends who were also invited to this party. She doubted they had met any of them before; people seem to come and go in her life fairly quickly, with no reason for them to be introduced to her parents. Old friends that remembered school trips and prom were in short supply these days.

But then Mum and Dad were usually fairly laid-back when it came to meeting new people. She doubted they would stay late – but she knew they'd booked a hotel room nearby. And perhaps they could go for a nice breakfast – or more probably, lunch – on the Monday, to make up for the fact that Macy was sure she would not spend an awful lot of time with them at the party.

Feeling excited and a little apprehensive about the big birthday bash, Macy decided to head to bed before midnight – which was fairly unusual for her – and get a decent night's sleep. Tomorrow would be the last day of her twenties and it felt somewhat momentous.

Something was wrong. She knew that as soon she opened her eyes on the last day that she would be twenty-nine years old. The pain in her head throbbed like nothing she had known before and she was unsure whether she could make it to the kitchen to get a glass of water to take some paracetamol.

She had suffered with headaches before – fairly regularly, especially when she was stressed. But nothing like this. It was a struggle to even open her eyes, and so she left them closed and willed herself to go back to sleep. Had she been drinking the night before, she might've thought it was a hangover – but the most she had had was a cup of tea and a chocolate biscuit. Nothing that should be causing a headache like this. Perhaps she had not had enough sleep, she thought. Maybe if she could doze off once more, she would wake up and feel totally better. This was not how she wanted to spend today. A precious day off, and her birthday party the following day. She did not want to spend it in bed feeling miserable, especially with no good reason.

Half an hour later, when she opened her eyes once

more, the pain had not dissipated. If anything it was worse, and she knew she could not avoid getting up and taking some painkillers. But as she sat up she realised with even more clarity that this was not a normal headache.

Her eyes felt like they were spinning inside her skull, and she was pretty sure she was swaying, for remaining upright seemed impossible. She tried to stand, took one step and stumbled, and then crawled towards the bathroom, wanting to cry, wanting to scream, but not knowing if anything would help. And then, suddenly, a rush of nausea – and she emptied her guts all over the hallway floor.

"Help," she croaked, but of course there was no one to hear her. That was the problem with living alone.

What was happening? She could not see straight, could not walk, could not stop being sick, and the pain in her head made her want to rip open her skull just to stop the throbbing.

She needed help.

But who could she ask? And what could they even do? What was this? A headache? Some sort of sickness bug? Some terrible disease? A brain tumour, perhaps? No. That was a dangerous path to go down. Diagnosing one's own symptoms always led to certain mortality.

So she did the only thing that seemed possible,

and crawled back to her bed, yanking her phone from the bedside table where it was charging, and dialling 999.

"Ambulance, please," she got out, before vomiting all over the floor, and one of her legs.

Never in her life had Macy felt so alone. A and E was busy, unsurprisingly, and no-one seemed to grasp quite how ill she felt - no matter how many times she vomited, or told them she thought she was going to die. The paramedics had started some sort of IV, and checked her blood pressure - and yet here she was, huddled in a wheelchair in the busy A and E, vomiting into a bowl and wondering how long she was going to be left there.

She wished someone was with her, if only to stop her panicking so much, or to go and ask how long she would wait to be seen - but there was no-one. Who could she call? None of her friends were close enough to her that she would ring them for something like this - and it would take her parents well over an hour to get here, and they would only panic. After all, it was probably just a dodgy prawn or something, messing with her system.

At least, that's what she tried to tell herself, as she sat there, watching the world going by and feeling like she didn't even have the energy to cry. The pain in her head was horrendous, the vomiting disgusting - but it wasn't just that. Her vision was a little more normal now, although not as sharp as she remembered. But her whole body just felt wrong. She felt as though she was not even well enough to sit there, in the wheelchair, to even exist… but there was no-one to even try to explain that confusing concept to, because she was left to wait.

She tried to take some comfort from that. The paramedics who had brought her in obviously didn't think it was that severe, whatever it was, because surely someone would have seen her by now if that was the case?

"Do you want some water, Miss?" a man's voice asked, and with difficulty, Macy lifted her head just high enough to see who was speaking. An older man, with short grey hair and a scruffy white beard was the one who had addressed her - and although water sounded like a good plan, she did not accept.

"No, thank you," she managed to say. She wondered if the police officers cuffed to either side of the man would have allowed him to get her a drink, if she had accepted. Why had he offered, she wondered? Because he cared about this woman all alone, terrified she was going to die in this waiting room? Or because he wanted a reason to move, to escape his jailers, to make them move…

At least he wasn't alone.

The minutes ticked by, but it felt like all concept of time had disappeared to Macy. It could have been minutes or hours later when a nurse called out her name; for a second, she almost forgot to respond.

"Here," she said finally, giving a weak wave. "Sorry, I can't walk…" She just knew that if she tried standing again, she would end up on the floor - and anyway, as the nurse came and took a rough hold of the wheelchair handles, Macy vomited into an already rather full sick bowl once more. She considered apologising, but didn't have the energy, and so kept her mouth shut.

Finally, she was wheeled into the inner sanctum, behind the curtain that earlier patients had been called behind. They reached a pale wooden door, and the wheelchair stopped.

"The wheelchair won't fit in the room," she nurse said. "You'll have to walk."

"I'll fall…" Macy said, taken aback by the brusque nature of the nurse while she sat so vulnerable, feeling so ill.

"You'll make it," the nurse said, taking the sick bowl from her lap and opening the door. Macy stood, shakily, and stumbled in, keeping low for fear of falling, and immediately collapsing into the chair next to the desk. It was no more comfortable than the wheelchair, and all she wanted to do was lie down, but there was another nurse here, and she only hoped this was a step in the right direction.

"Hello, Miss Maxwell. I'm Nurse Cranford, can you tell me why you're here today?"

"I think I'm dying," Macy said, tears rolling down her cheeks, as she reached out and gripped the desk. "Please, I feel so ill, I'm going to be sick-"

And then the first nurse returned, thrusting a clean sick bowl at her, and once more Macy emptied the contents of her stomach.

She tried the best she could to explain everything that had happened, all while wishing that the pain in her head could ease just a little. Surely soon someone would actually help her?

"We'll get you to a more comfortable chair," the nurse was saying, although the words seemed very far away. "And a doctor will come and see you."

"Please don't let me die," Macy whispered, and the nurse reached out and squeezed her hand.

"We won't. You're in the right place now, Macy, I promise. Now, Nurse Smith will wheel you to the assessment area."

And then, just like that, the wheelchair was in the room - and Macy almost fell into it, before throwing up yet again.

Could they not see how ill she was? Or was her mind simply playing tricks on her? Was this nothing, as they all seemed to be pretending it was?

She could only hope so.

The next chair she fell into did at least recline. She felt like even sitting up was too much effort. The pain in her head had not subsided, and as they put in a cannula - which under normal circumstances would probably have caused her a decent amount of anxiety, but now was simply something she had to deal with - she hoped they could give her something for the pain soon.

And, she thought as she emptied her stomach yet again, something for the vomiting.

She lost count of how many doctors and nurses she spoke to. Finally some medication from a drip stopped her vomiting, but the paracetamol offered wasn't really cutting through the pain. Even existing seemed to hurt, and the black cloud of death did not disappear from her mind. Something terrible was wrong, she was sure - but no-one seemed to know what.

Eventually sleep seemed to come, and it was the

only relief she'd had in hours - but then someone came to wake her up, and check her vitals, and the hell started all over again.

She realised she should probably tell someone where she was, but the thought of even looking at her phone made her want to be sick, in spite of the medication running through her veins to stop that.

"Miss Maxwell?" a young doctor asked, pulling aside the curtain. "How are you feeling? I'm Doctor Jennet."

"Not good," she said, trying to sit up but finding it a challenge.

"Is it the worst headache you have ever had? I see here that you have suffered from migraines before."

"The worst ever," she said. "And I just feel so ill…"

He nodded. "Can you scrunch your eyes tight? Now open them. Now can you squeeze my hands, as tight as you can? Okay, pull me in, now push me away…"

It carried on for some minutes, with tasks that weren't difficult to accomplish but did not help Macy's terrible headache.

"Is there anything else I can take for the pain?" she asked, when he seemed to be done with her for now.

"I'll have a look into it," he promised.

She nodded dolefully, and then once again she was alone, trying to take comfort in the fact that no-one seemed too worried.

But then why did she feel so terrible?

Eight hours had passed since she had entered A and E, by the time a decision was made, and she still had not felt well enough to look at her phone. The large analogue clock on the wall, however, told her that most of the day had gone, and yet she was still here, and still wondering what was making her feel so rotten.

"Miss Maxwell," the doctor said, almost announcing himself with her name as he drew the curtain open. "I have spoken with the other doctors, and believe you are suffering from a migraine. There is no suggestion that you need any scans - just plenty of rest at home."

"A migraine?"

He nodded.

"They can be this bad?" Relief washed over her, and then disbelief. She had suffered from migraines before, in her teenage years - and never had she felt anything like this.

"They can be, yes."

"How long will it last?"

"It can be up to three days," he said. "But hopefully not that long. Keep taking paracetamol, plenty of fluids, and rest."

"And if it doesn't go away?"

"I'm sure it will," he said, with far more confidence than Macy could muster to believe him. "But if it gets worse, or your experience any numbness or loss of function or vision, then come back here."

She nodded, struggling to take it all in. How was she going to go home, feeling like this? Although the thought of sleeping for twelve hours straight in her own bed was a lovely one. But the pain… in her head, her neck, her whole body. If she felt well enough, perhaps a bath would have been nice - but she wasn't sure how she would get up the stairs at home, let alone get in a bath.

"Is there anyone at home to keep any eye on you?"

She shook her head, and felt tears threatening to overwhelm her. It had been a very long day, and the following day was her thirtieth birthday - and here she was, alone and feeling more ill than she had ever felt in her life.

"Perhaps you might want to call a friend," he said. "Ask them to pop in and check on you…"

She nodded, before realising how painful that was, and stopped.

"I'll get your discharge paperwork sorted, and then you're free to go," he said.

How could leaving hospital be such an unappealing thought?

At least it was only a migraine, she thought; that was a comfort. It would pass; nothing had given them any cause for concern, and she had seen enough doctors and nurses for someone to pick up on any problem, surely?

A friend she could call to check up on her… that was a bit more challenging. She needed a lift home, really - the thought of a taxi was not appealing in that moment, and besides, they probably weren't that keen on picking up people from A and E. She was concerned the vomiting might start again, and then she'd have even more problems to deal with today.

There was Lucy, from work - perhaps she would be willing to help out. Or Alex - but she'd had a fling with him the previous summer, and so things were a bit more awkward now. Or maybe Toni, from next door; yes, she was the best choice, for at least she would only have to drive home. And maybe she had noticed the ambulance, and was concerned for her next-door-neighbour slash friend?

For the first time since ringing the ambulance, Macy pulled out her phone.

No messages.

No missed calls.

She sighed; at least no-one was sat at home, panicking about her, she thought.

Talking seemed like too much effort, but as she typed out a message, she realised the migraine was interfering with her ability to spell, and to think of the right words. Eventually though, she had a message that was understandable, and hit send, hoping Toni had her phone in sight.

*Had terrible migraine. In hospital. Any chance you could pick me up? Would really appreciate it. Thanks. M x*

A reply came seconds later, and Macy forced her eyes to focus on the words. At least her vision seemed better now.

*OMG hun are you ok? Of course! Shall I leave now?*

Hunched over and struggling to believe she could still feel so ill and be sent home, Macy staggered to the front of the hospital, and leant against the wall as she waited for Toni to arrive. It was evening now, and the air was cool, but it was a welcome change from the stuffiness of the hospital. Beside her, a man in a hospital gown pushing around a drip stand was lighting a cigarette. He was accompanied by a nurse, and Macy wondered if he wasn't really well enough to be out here. The smell of the smoke did not help her headache, but she did not have the energy to move away from it.

A siren wailed nearby, and Macy focussed on keeping herself upright. At least she would be home soon, and could sleep off this migraine. Then perhaps she could find something to ease it. Surely the pain couldn't last much longer? She had never had a migraine before that had not responded to painkillers or sleep… hopefully this one would become more typical soon.

Toni's blue Citroen pulled up in the layby in front of her, and Macy made her way to the door, wincing at every movement.

"Hi," she said, her voice sounding a little distant. "Thanks for coming."

"No problem. I couldn't believe you were in the hospital! You know, I thought I heard an ambulance this morning, but I had a heavy night last night and slept it off. And with your birthday party tomorrow! What a nightmare. You must be better though, if they're sending you home, right?"

"I don't feel great," Macy managed to say, as the river of words began again. The noise was making her feel worse, and she felt like asking Toni to be quiet - but knew that it would be rude to do so. Instead she focussed on breathing in and out, and on not vomiting. It was only a ten minute drive, she could do this…

Or she hoped she could.

"Are you going to be all right on your own tonight?" Toni asked as they pulled up in the car park for their block of flats. "I can come over, if you like…" Her tone suggested she would rather not, and thankfully, despite how ill she was feeling, she did not fancy Toni's company either.

"I'll be okay," she said. "I'll ring you, if I get worse."

"If you're sure," Toni said. "I'm still hanging from last night…"

Macy didn't have the energy to respond as she got out of the car and slowly walked towards the front door. There was no lift, but thankfully she was only on the first floor - although the stairs took three times the amount of time to ascend as they would have normally done.

Her hand shook as she put the key in the lock, and tears threatened to overwhelm her. This was too much. She felt too ill. Even knowing what the problem was, she still felt scared about what was happening to her. Perhaps she had some frozen peas in, she thought, to put on her neck, on her head, t0 ease this pain a bit.

"I need to lie down," she said abruptly to Toni. "Thanks."

"No problem!" Toni said, all too chirpily. "Ring me if you need me!"

Macy shut the door and decide the bed was too far. Falling onto the sofa as soon as she reached it, she pulled the blanket that was always somewhere nearby over her and closed her eyes.

Please, please, make it stop, she thought to herself.

When she next woke up, Macy forgot for a moment where she was and what had happened. But the pain was still there, and when she sat she felt dizzy, and all the memories of the day spent in hospital came flooding back.

Her mouth was dry and she thought a drink might help her head, so she staggered into the kitchen and let the tap run until the water was cool and clear. And that was when she saw it: the clock on the microwave, its bright green digital numbers informing her it was 03:24am.

*Happy Birthday to me* she thought, as she downed some water and winced at the pain moving her neck caused. Every step felt like a trial, but she managed to find a bag of frozen peas in the freezer, wrap a tea towel round them and hold them to the back of her head where the pain was worse, before finally making it to her bed. The duvet felt cool against her skin and her eyes closed as soon as her head touched the pillow.

She was thirty years old, with a party that evening, and at the minute the idea of dragging herself to the bathroom was too difficult.

What a bad start.

Constant beeping from her phone, where she had abandoned it in the living room, eventually woke her again, but she was not surprised this time that the pain had not subsided. When she sat up, the world seemed to shimmer before her, and so for a few moments she sat and waited until it felt safe to stand. It wasn't as bad as when she had called the ambulance, at least; she had not been sick again, nor felt like her eyes were rolling around inside her head. She wasn't better… but she wasn't worse, either.

Her phone was almost dead, wedged between the sofa cushions from when she had collapsed there upon coming home the evening before, but it had enough battery for her to flick through all the messages that were causing the beeping.

*Happy Birthday!*

*The big 3-0! Can't wait to party tonight. X*

*Happy birthday old lady! X*

She held her head in her hands, and let the tears she had been holding in flow free. She was cold, but the heating was too far away right now. She felt weak, but food was too far away.

There was no way she was going to be well enough for this party tonight.

So she did the only thing she could think of, and picked up her phone, dialling the only person she wanted around her right now.

"Mum?" she said, as soon as the call connected. "Mum, I feel so ill."

"Oh, sweetheart," Mum said, as soon as Macy managed to open the door. "You look terrible. Happy birthday, by the way."

"Thanks, Mum. I feel terrible…"

"Did you drink last night? It's not a hangover is it?" Dad asked, looking the up and down.

Macy slumped in the chair, finding standing to be

too difficult. If she were honest, sitting felt too much like hard work – but lying in bed wasn't making anything any better either.

She shook her head. "No, I didn't drink anything last night. Haven't in a few nights actually." Somewhere inside she felt a sense of indignation that anyone could think she would be this ill with a hangover, but she didn't have the energy to sustain the feeling.

"Just checking," Dad said, as Mum tutted.

"I'll go make a drink, and something to eat – and then you can tell us all about it, Macy. You need something to give you some energy, maybe some painkillers, too."

"Thanks, Mum," Macy said, letting her eyes drift closed. She was vaguely aware of her father sitting down next to her, but conversation felt like too much effort right now.

"Never seen you have a migraine this bad," Dad said.

"Never felt one this bad," Macy said, through gritted teeth. The pain was definitely still there, and the nausea – but then she didn't really remember when she had last eaten, so perhaps that was the issue. At least Mum and Dad were here now. She couldn't even bring herself to care about the party that she knew Mum had quickly cancelled as they drove down here. None of it seemed important compared with how ill she felt. She was sure, in a day or two, she would feel totally normal, and be gutted that her thirtieth birthday had been ruined by this inconvenient migraine.

But for now all she felt was pain and despair.

# CHAPTER TWO

In the end, almost the entirety of Macy's thirtieth birthday was spent in bed. She tried to sit and chat with her parents, but it was too difficult - and she ended up turning off her mobile when she realised so many of the texts were about people's disappointment in the cancelling of her party, and not because they were concerned about her health.

"Sweetheart?" Mum said, as opened the door and slipped in. "Do you need anything?"

"I just want the pain to go away," Macy said, voice thick with tears, and she felt the bed dip as her mother sat down.

"It will," Mum said. "Soon, I'm sure. The doctors wouldn't have sent you home if they were worried."

"I suppose," Macy said.

"Do you want something to eat?"

"I can't face it."

"Drink?"

"Maybe some water… can you see if you can find a straw? I think there's one in the second drawer. I'm not sure I can lift my head long enough."

Mum gave her a sad look, and then left to fulfil her requests.

When Macy woke up again, the dark skies and the alarm clock on her bedside table told her it was no longer her birthday.

Somehow she had lost the whole exciting day of turning thirty to this horrendous migraine. She could never get it back; it felt like it should have been a momentous moment in her life's story, and yet it had faded away without really even being marked.

And yet… she thought she wouldn't care about that if she could just stop feeling so damn ill.

The flat was quiet, and she presumed her parents had gone to the hotel room they had booked for the night of her birthday party - but when she went out to go to the bathroom, Mum was sprawled on the sofa asleep, and Dad was on pillows on the floor. She moved away quickly, so as not to wake them, but felt bad that they were so uncomfortable for her.

Were they worried about leaving her alone?

She had to admit, she did not want to be left alone;

she didn't feel well enough to be out of hospital, let alone left by herself. But she didn't want to inconvenience her parents…

Once she was back in her quiet and dark bedroom, she found that in spite of how drained she felt, she could not sleep. Perhaps there were only so many hours in the day a body could sleep, no matter how ill they were. Still she did not feel up to doing anything - and it was the middle of the night - but there was one task that had to be accomplished. She felt sure that she would not be well enough to work by the time the sun rose that day, and so she quickly typed an email to let her line manager know, hoping he would pick it up in time before assuming she was just late. She was sure they would think she was skiving, perhaps hungover after her birthday - but the colleagues she had invited could surely attest to the fact that the party had been cancelled due to her ill health.

*Hi Mike. Sorry to email but I have been in hospital this weekend and will not be well enough to work tomorrow. I will keep you informed.*

*Thanks,*

*Macy*

Mike didn't like her anyway, so Macy was sure he would find this a good reason to despise her further - but it felt a weight off her shoulders to know she did not have to get up and try to get dressed, let alone sit up all day in a busy office with all the noise and clatter and expectations.

The doctors said a few days and she would be back to normal - so even if she had to call in sick the rest of the week, she was confident that by Monday she would be well enough to work again. And this would all be an unfortunate blip at the beginning of her thirties.

"Macy," Mum said, coming in with a cup of tea. "I think you should ring the doctors…"

"They said it would go off…"

"It's been two full days of you lying in bed, and you're no better. And you're still dizzy…"

"I guess. I just…"

"Ring them - you'll need a sick note for work anyway, if it carries on, right?"

Macy nodded. The idea of talking on the phone felt too much, but if she were honest, she had started to think she needed to speak to someone again. Dad had gone to the hotel room the second night, but Mum had stayed on the sofa again - and Macy knew this couldn't go on indefinitely. They were supposed to have gone back home today - but Macy didn't think she was well enough to be left alone, and neither did her mother.

She tried not to think about how quiet her phone had been since she had turned it back on. Her friends obviously thought she was fine - for none of them seemed to consider checking in. Even Toni next door hadn't knocked to see if she was all right now - but then, thought Macy, perhaps she had seen Macy's parents arriving and hadn't wanted to disturb.

"Can you come into the surgery this afternoon?" the doctor asked, after a phone appointment that morning.

"I'm not sure I feel well enough" Macy admitted, sipping a cup of tea her mum had brought her, but feeling very much like she might just bring it back up again. The nausea had never completely subsided, although thankfully she had not vomited again since her day in A and E. "Can you give me something for the pain?"

"I can…" the doctor said, her voice sounding a little unsure. "But if you don't feel right by Friday, I want to see you - I don't want you leaving this over the weekend, all right?"

Macy agreed, and soon her Dad was fetching the prescription for pain relief. It would be gone by Friday, she was sure; and she couldn't imagine what the GP could check her for that the hospital had not.

❖ ❖ ❖

Mum sat beside her in the doctor's waiting room, on hard plastic chairs that were definitely not designed for sitting for any length of time. It was Friday morning, and Macy had to admit she still wasn't feeling right. The dizziness, the pain, the nausea; none had gone away completely, and at some points seemed to return with a vengeance.

She felt bad that Mum was still here, sleeping on her sofa, although Dad had returned home to get back to work and sleep in his own bed - but Macy couldn't help but feel relieved that this time she was not on her own.

Until she had fallen ill, she had not realised how lonely her existence had been.

"Miss Macy Maxwell to Room 3, please," the electronic voice said, and Macy stood, Mum at her side. She felt a bit like a child, being accompanied by her mum to the doctors - but she found she didn't care. She needed the support.

"Hello, Macy," the doctor - a man this time, and not one she had seen before - said. "Can you tell me what's been happening? I can see you were in A and E last weekend…"

And so, with occasional interruptions by Mum, Macy began to explain how ill she had been feeling. "I'm sure it's just a migraine," she said, for the third or fourth time. "But the doctors seem to think it would be gone by now and, well, it's not. I just feel so drained…"

The doctor nodded, and glanced at his computer, then back at her. "Can you just walk across the room for me, in a straight line?" She did so, and presumed she passed whatever test, as he didn't say anything more. "Now squeeze my hands. Pull them back, push them away…" She followed all the instructions without a pause; this was not, after all, the first time she had been through this examination.

"Everything seems normal…" he said. "I'll check your blood pressure, and your temperature…"

When both were normal, he seemed a little flummoxed.

"I'd like to call the hospital, if that's all right - just to see what they would advise, considering how long this is lasting. If you could wait in the waiting room, I'll come out as soon as I've spoken to them."

Back in the hard plastic chairs, Macy reached out and squeezed Mum's hand.

"What if it's something terrible?" she asked, voicing that fear that had been in her mind since that moment she had woken up and struggled to stay upright.

"It won't be," Mum said, but there was a bit of

a wobble in her voice. "You were checked out by loads of doctors at the hospital. It'll just be some unusual migraine, or a virus or something."

The doctor reappeared before Macy could respond. "The neurologist would like to see you," he said. "I think we can bypass A and E this time - if you go to the Acute Medical Unit this afternoon, he'll see you."

Macy nodded, but said nothing. It was Mum that asked the questions.

"A neurologist? Why? What do you think is wrong?"

"Nothing, I'm sure - but better to get everything checked out."

"Will they scan her? Surely she needs some sort of scan?"

"They may well do - but I can't speculate, I'm afraid. I must get back to my patients, Mrs Maxwell, I apologise…"

"Of course, of course," Mum said, waving her hand and taking a deep breath. "Come on Macy. It'll be fine - we'll get you all checked out, and then maybe you come home with me for a few days to recuperate from this, hey? I can make you all your favourite meals - and that doctor at least gave you a sick note for a couple of weeks."

Macy nodded. "That sounds nice."

"Come on then - let's get to that hospital and get this done. Nothing is ever quick in hospital, is it!"

❖ ❖ ❖

As Mum had predicted, it was not quick. They sat in chairs not much more comfortable than those in the doctors' waiting room, and barely ate or drank for the rest of the day. The waiting room was freezing, and Macy leant against her Mum and wished she'd thought to bring a coat. How nice it would be to be at home, under her duvet, instead of here, waiting to be poked and prodded by yet another doctor. How had a perfectly normal evening turned into a week of feeling like this? Suddenly hospitals and doctors were becoming her norm.

When she eventually saw the doctor, it was all the same: questions, hand squeezing, walking in a straight line. All the things that had been fine on Sunday in hospital - so why would they be a problem now?

"Okay, Macy. I think we need to rule out viral meningitis - so I need to do a lumbar puncture. Also, this can help us see if you have an aneurysm in your brain."

"Aneurysm?"

"Lumbar puncture?"

Both Mum and Macy spoke at the same time; the doctor addressed Macy first. "If we do a CT scan, it may not show issues clearly from a week ago. So a lumbar puncture is more accurate."

"I don't want a lumbar puncture," Macy said. "I feel so ill already, and I don't like needles, and… what happens if it is viral meningitis?"

"We don't treat it - it should resolve itself in time."

"Can we do a scan instead?"

The doctor sighed; Macy knew she wasn't making things simple, but the fear she felt about having a lumbar puncture was almost worse than how ill she felt.

Almost.

"We could do a CT with a contrast dye - but it won't be as accurate."

She shivered. She still didn't like the thought of the needle that would be needed for the dye - but it least it sounded better than a lumbar puncture. "I understand," Macy said.

"And if it's an aneurysm?" Mum said, her voice shaking.

"Then we will need to talk again - because that definitely will need to be dealt with. I'll put through the order for the CT now - they'll come and get you when they're ready."

Macy nodded, a million questions and worries racing through her mind, and grabbed Mum's arm for support.

"Come on," she said, helping her from the room. "It will be all right. They're just checking to make sure nothing is missed."

Macy nodded, and tried to stop a sob escaping from her throat, but failed.

"Shh, it's all right. You're freezing - here, I'll go and get us a cup of tea, okay? You stay here, in case they call you.

Macy nodded again, and leant her head back against the wall. Was this all an overreaction to a migraine? Or was this the beginning of the end of her story? She wasn't done living yet...

❖ ❖ ❖

"We'll just get this cannula in for the contrast, and then you're all set for the CT," the young nurse said. He was wearing a pink scrub top, and Macy wondered if that signified anything, or whether it was just the colour he had put on - but it seemed different to the others around him. She was trying to focus on anything really, other than the worries about what was wrong with her.

Could the doctors have missed something terrible back in A and E?

"Sharp scratch," the nurse said, and Macy took a deep breath and looked at her mum instead of the needle.

"Hmmm," the nurse said, and it wasn't a confident sound.

"Everything all right?" Mum asked, and Macy was glad someone else was there to ask the questions.

"Just struggling to get the cannula in — your veins aren't playing ball, Macy," he said. "You feel a bit cold…"

Macy nodded. "It was freezing in the waiting room."

The nurse nodded. "I'm just going to get my colleague to have a try…"

An older nurse, female this time and in a dark blue scrub top - but yet again lots of sighs. Macy winced at another unsuccessful jab.

"I can't find any good veins," she said, glancing at both arms. One had a tourniquet tightly tied around it; the other was littered with the signs of failed attempts.

"If you fill a glove with hot water, we'll try warming her arm up a bit," she said to the other nurse. "I'm going to call for an ultrasound," she said to Macy. "They can use it to find a good vein, to put the cannula in."

"Okay," Macy said in a quiet voice, glancing at the big clock on the wall. The sky outside was growing dusky, and time was ticking on. Another full day spent chasing answers, and still she felt no better. If anything, she felt worse, after all the needles that had been shoved in her arms.

How nice it would be to be at home, in her bed, with a cup of tea… but then she wouldn't know what was wrong with her, and that wouldn't solve things at all.

The warm balloon-glove felt quite nice after hours of being cold, although it looked rather silly - but Macy found she didn't have the energy to laugh at it.

"Hi, Macy," another voice said, and Macy looked up and forced a smile. "I'm Bridget, an ultrasound technician. I'm just going to have a look and see what veins we can find to use for this cannula, okay?"

Macy nodded again; she'd had enough of all these people poking and prodding her body, but she supposed they had to.

"Have you eaten much today? Or drunk much?" she asked.

Macy shook her head.

"There's no veins here that will be big enough for the cannula you need," she said, with a sigh and a furrowed brow, before handing her a tissue to wipe off the ultrasound gel that was covering both arms. "Let me speak with the doctor, and see what the alternative is."

"Okay," Macy said, feeling like her voice, along with her energy, was fading away. Nothing was going to plan…

◆ ◆ ◆

She and Mum sat in silence while they waited, neither wanting to voice their concerns, but neither having the brain capacity to discuss anything other than the predicament Macy found herself in.

"Macy Maxwell," the doctor said as he approached, a clipboard in his hand. "So, the cannula isn't going to work…"

"Can you do the scan without it?" Macy asked hopefully.

"I'm afraid not," the doctor said. "We need the contrast to show up anything that might have been happening for the last week. Without it we won't get a conclusive picture. So instead, we'll do an MRI scan."

"Okay," Macy said, thinking at least that wouldn't involve more needles.

"But," the doctor said, and Macy's heart dropped. "It's late in the day now, so it won't be until tomorrow."

"We've been here all day, doctor," Mum said. "Is there no way…"

"I can ask, but I highly doubt it. Now, we can admit you…"

"Am I safe to go home?" Macy asked, knowing that a night in hospital was the last thing she wanted.

"I believe so. Although if it is an aneurysm, then it could rupture at any time…"

"With respect," Macy said, finally feeling some energy to argue her point. "I've been at home feeling like this for a week. And something could have happened at any time then…"

"True. If you want to go home, I won't argue - if you can be back here at 9am for the MRI."

"She'll be here," Mum said.

And then he was gone, and Macy didn't know how she was going to deal with another night of feeling so ill, and all this uncertainty.

"Come on love," Mum said, taking her arm and steering her out of the ward. "Let's go home, and have something nice for dinner. It will all look better in the morning."

But would it? Macy was finding it harder and harder to believe.

❖ ❖ ❖

"She's got to go back for an MRI in the morning," Macy heard her mum say on the phone to her dad. "So they can see if they can figure out what's going on."

They had eaten dinner - well, Macy had picked at some fried rice from the local Chinese takeaway - and watched something on telly, before Macy had said she needed an early night. She felt bad her mum was still sleeping on the sofa, but she had declined when Macy had offered to swap.

"I'm worried, Joe," she heard her mum say, and that set her heart racing. Mum always seemed so calm, so capable, so unflappable…

"I know, I know. But what if…" And then Macy thought she heard tears, and so she buried her head under the pillow and wished all this away. It was hard enough living through it; she couldn't cope with her mum being upset about it too.

At least by tomorrow she should have some answers, she thought. And then hopefully a plan to fix whatever was wrong with her.

✦ ✦ ✦

"Have you had an MRI before?" the technician asked, when she was finally called in for her scan, after waiting for two hours in the Acute Medicine Unit again. Being a Saturday, the place had seemed much quieter - but that also seemed to mean things were a lot slower.

Macy shook her head.

"Okay," the woman said, a kindly smile on her face, her blonde curls bobbing as she spoke. "Well, it's very loud, but we'll put headphones on you. And you'll have a button to call us if you need to. It's not enclosed, you just move in and out of it - but you'll need to stay still, okay? It'll take about twenty-five minutes."

Macy nodded, trying to take it all in.

"And you don't have any metal in your body? Or anything in your pockets?"

Macy shook her head. "There might be underwire in my bra…"

"That's fine. You might feel it pull away slightly but it won't be a problem. Now, if you get yourself lying down - careful, the headrest is a bit hard - and we'll get started."

With the headphones on, the noise inside the

machine was still enough to make her headache worse. Macy hadn't realised how noisy they were; so old and clunky, and yet such an expensive and important test.

As she tried very hard to stay still, she thought about all the things she had ignored the past week. Work - who were nagging her about a sick note. Her friends - who had stopped messaging, although not many of them had messaged to begin with. The painting that she had been working on.

She had always loved to paint, although she wasn't sure she was very good. But over the years she had practised doing portraits - from memory, or photos, never with live models - and she fancied she was improving. Not that she let anyone see them. She had tried landscapes, but they had never really turned out right.

Her latest was a self-portrait; something she had felt was apt for the year she was turning thirty. But now it sat in her desk, forgotten and unloved. Her vision was still feeling a bit fuzzy, which she presumed was due to whatever was wrong with her - and she didn't think she could paint properly until it returned to normal.

She just hoped everything would return to normal soon.

◆ ◆ ◆

More waiting. Somehow, this week had turned into days and days of pain and waiting.

Once again, mum went to get a cup of tea, but Macy's went largely un-drunk. Her foot tapped on the grey floor as she waited and waited and waited. They said the doctor would speak with her once the results of the test were in. Would it be the same doctor as yesterday? She hadn't thought to ask. Perhaps because it was a weekend, it would be someone different. She almost hoped so, for she had felt that the man yesterday had found her rather a pain, and had seemed rather dismissive of quite how ill she felt.

There were only two other people waiting this time. Some sort of clinic ran from here on a weekend, she had heard people saying – but she wasn't quite sure what it was for. The manic rushing around of the week days had gone; but in its place, was a sense that no one was in any hurry to solve Macy's problem.

"Miss Maxwell?" A woman with short cropped hair called out, and Macy raised her hand. Mum had gone to the bathroom, but Macy thought she would figure out where she had gone; she could send a text as soon as she knew what was happening.

The woman – who introduced herself as Dr Jamieson – was accompanied by a younger woman with long curly hair and a clipboard, and yet another young woman in a nurse's uniform. As soon as Macy sat down on the reclining chair she was offered, the nurse began flashing a light in her eyes and muttering about pupil responses.

Macy's heart began to race, and she wished she'd waited for Mum to get back.

"Has anyone talked to you about your test results?" the doctor asked, pulling a curtain around her.

"No...but you're scaring me a bit now," Macy said. Why did three people need to tell her what was on her MRI? And why had they taken her off in private? And why had they drawn the curtain? Was she dying? Were they about to tell her she had weeks to live? The tension was unbearable.

"You don't need to be scared, Miss Maxwell," the doctor said. "But I have looked at your MRI, and there is a significant area of damage. It seems that you've had a stroke sometime within the last week."

A stroke?

Surely they must be wrong.

"Now," said the doctor. "It says here that you were admitted to A and E with head pain, nausea and vertigo last week. I would assume that is what happened."

"I'm only thirty..." Macy said. "I've literally just turned thirty. How does this happen?"

"I know it's a shock. Is somebody here with you?"

Macy nodded and at that moment heard her mum calling her name. The nurse went out to show her the way and when mum entered the curtained off area, a sob escaped Macy's throat.

"Macy, what is it? What's wrong?"

"Mum. Mum, they're saying I've had a stroke."

❖ ❖ ❖

"We never would have sent you home if we'd known you'd had a stroke," the younger of the two doctors was saying, and internally, Macy was screaming.

"They sent her home while she was having the bloody stroke," Mum said, and then apologised for her language.

"Will... will I recover?"

"We'll know more once we've done some more scans," the doctor said. "But yes, you should do. There may be some residual issues, and we need to find out why someone like you - young, with no medical issues, is having a stroke. Meanwhile there's medications we need you to take, to prevent this happening again. My colleague will go through it all with you."

Macy nodded, but she was barely listening to a word they said.

A stroke.

The words ran through her mind over and over, making her feel sicker than she already did. When they took her for yet another scan, she stood and nearly passed out - and this time she was wheeled to the MRI machine. No longer did she have the confidence that she would walk away from this unchanged.

As she lay in the machine with the headphones on once more, she focussed on trying very hard not to cry.

*I don't want to die.*

*I'm not ready for this to be it.*

The thoughts wouldn't go away, but she knew if she gave into them, if she started crying now, she might never stop.

They just needed to find the cause of the stroke, and fix it - and maybe then things would eventually be normal once more.

◆ ◆ ◆

Mum had talked all the way home, and although Macy was glad of the distraction, she found it was hard for it all to sink in.

They had offered to admit her, but had said that once she was on the statins and blood thinners, there wasn't much need - and she just wanted to be at home.

For a whole week she had been walking around, suffering the after-effects of a stroke, and had not had a clue. No-one had.

And now they didn't even know what had caused it.

They had done another scan, looking for a reason, but none had been found. Medical words were thrown around, and Macy was glad Mum was there, for she would have paid more attention to it all. All Macy really remembered was that she had had a stroke, that a reason was not yet obvious, but that they were sure that they would find one. And that the sickness, dizziness, headaches, vision problems should subside. And the exhaustion, and a whole list of other problems that she may not well have noticed yet.

It should all improve, in time, they said - but they didn't seem sure on when.

Or why this had happened. Or how.

A twinge in Macy's chest had her panicking instantly: was this how she was going to feel now? Terrified whenever she had a pain anywhere?

Constantly worrying that she was about to drop down dead?

"Are you all right?" Mum asked, as they pulled up in the car park. Dad had taken their car home, but thankfully Mum was happy enough driving Macy's little Corsa.

"No," Macy said truthfully. "I just... I think I'm in shock."

Mum nodded. "Me too. Let's get upstairs, then we can talk about it - and I'll run out and get that prescription for you, so you can start it tonight."

"The doctor said I could start tomorrow, now I have the aspirin," Macy said.

"I know. But you'll feel better if you start it tonight."

Macy nodded. "Why has this happened, Mum?" she asked, tears building in her eyes.

Mum reached over and squeezed her hand. "I don't know love. But we'll get through it. You're strong, and you're in good shape, and the doctors will figure out what's going on. Now, let's get you in, and get the kettle on."

# CHAPTER THREE

It was all decided in a couple of days, really. For two days Macy didn't let Mum leave the house: she just couldn't face being alone. Every time she stood up she felt dizzy, and the high dose statins left her aching like she was a hundred years old.

She stopped locking the bathroom door, in case she collapsed overnight; and as she lay in bed struggling to sleep, she heard Mum coming in to secretly check on her.

She rang work on the Monday, and explained the situation, and that she would have a sick note from the doctor sent to them - but that they were probably talking about weeks, not days.

Her boss was sympathetic but functional; arranging practicalities with little sympathy.

When she text her group of friends, they were shocked, as she had expected: who heard of a thirty-year-old (well, she had been twenty-nine at the time, she supposed) having a stroke?

*Can't believe it. Let me know if you need anything! xx*

*OMG, that's mental. Here for you! xx*

*I'm shocked! How are you?*

She didn't really have the energy to reply, and she didn't feel like they would be that interested in the response anyway, so she left them for another day.

"Macy," Mum said, bringing in a bowl of soup and placing it in front of her. "Try to eat something."

"Even sitting here is exhausting," Macy said.

"I know. But you need to try to keep your energy up."

Macy nodded, and dipped some bread into the soup, mainly to appease her mother.

"I've been thinking. I don't think you should stay here, by yourself."

Macy nodded; she didn't want that either.

"Why don't you come back home for a few weeks? You're not working, we can take care of you, and you won't be alone."

She seemed like she was expecting an argument; Macy had always been very keen to be independent, supporting herself no matter what.

But Macy had no fight in her right now.

"Okay, Mum - if it's all right with you and Dad."

Mum wrapped her arms around Macy. "Of course it is! And your room basically hasn't changed since you left. This is for the best - I'm sure of it."

Macy was willing to trust her on that. She wanted someone to take charge of the situation - anything so she didn't have to.

◆ ◆ ◆

They decided to leave the next day: what was there to wait for? Mum was keen to get home, and the neurologists and the hospital hadn't sounded like they would be seeing Macy any time soon - and besides, she could always come back for appointments. It wasn't so far away, even though it had felt it when she had moved here.

Coming to a city alone after growing up in such a rural place had felt rather daring. Most of her school friends were still in the vicinity of the little Northumberland village where she had grown up - and yet she was the one who had gone off to live in the big city. She had been proud of that - and yet now, everything was crashing down around her.

She was so alone that her only option, when faced with this disaster, was to go back to her teenage bedroom.

She tried not to dwell on that.

Thinking she should probably let someone know

she was leaving, she dragged herself round to Toni's flat - and, thankfully, she was in.

"Hey! How are you feeling?" Toni asked, her hair tousled and her eyes a little bloodshot. Macy wondered if she'd been out drinking the night before.

"Not great," Macy said honestly, although she was beginning to wonder if anyone really wanted honesty when they asked that question.

"The migraine… it turns out it was a stroke," she said, the words still feeling strange in her mouth. "And I need some time to recover."

"Oh God, Mace! But your face hasn't dropped or anything, and you can walk… so was it, like, a mini stroke?"

Macy shook her head, then realised the action caused her pain. "No. Full on stroke - they're trying to figure out what happened."

"Well, at least you're okay."

Irritation coursed through her, because she very much was not okay - but she could not voice that to Toni. They weren't close enough.

"I'm going back up North, with my Mum," she said. "Until I'm better. Can I leave you with a key, in case there's any issues?"

Toni nodded. "Course. And if you need anything…"

Macy nodded, and walked away, feeling like she couldn't get away from there quick enough.

◆ ◆ ◆

"How are you feeling this morning?" Mum asked over breakfast, which Macy picked at.

"Dizzy," she said. "And everything hurts."

Mum reached over and squeezed her hand. "I'm sorry love. You'll feel better after some more rest. Have you got everything packed?"

Macy nodded. A large suitcase stood by the front door, but it wasn't even full. She had packed some clothes, toiletries, her laptop and her new batch of medications - but she didn't really need much for convalescing. She didn't pack any of her painting supplies, because her vision wasn't up to that - and it only made her more frustrated.

"Are you sure you're okay to drive my car that far?" Macy asked; one of the delightful side effects of having a stroke was not being able to drive for at least a month - not that she felt well enough to at the minute, anyway.

"I'll be fine," Mum said. "Do you need to see anyone before we go?"

Macy shook her head. "I've told Toni next door I'm going, and work. I'm not sure anyone cares, anyway."

"I'm sure that's not true, love," Mum said. "They probably just don't know how to handle all this."

Macy sighed and drained her tea, trying to ignore a pain in her head that was threatening to send her into a spiral of panic.

"Maybe. But if friends aren't around at the worst time in your life… what's the point?"

Mum didn't see to have an answer for that. "It will all get better, Macy, I promise you."

"I hope so," Macy said, feeling like a black cloud was consuming her. "I really hope so."

❖ ❖ ❖

"I'm going to be sick," Macy said, as they drove along the A1; thankfully it was not too busy, and Mum managed to pull into a lay-by before Macy emptied the contents of her stomach. It eased the nausea she'd been feeling for the entire drive, and as she climbed back into the passenger seat, she was pleased that Mum had thought to bring a bottle of water.

"All right?" Mum asked, sounding worried.

Macy nodded, even though she wasn't sure she'd ever be all right again.

She closed her eyes as they began to drive again,

listening to the radio softly murmuring in the background. It was mainly talking – a political debate of some sort, Macy thought, but she was finding it hard to follow anything at the moment.

Was this permanent? This difficulty with focusing? It felt like she was dragging her brain through setting concrete whenever she tried to focus on anything around her. And she hadn't tried anything more difficult than watching the telly, or making a cup of tea. How would she ever drive again?

There were so many questions she realised she hadn't asked the experts, but she hadn't felt well enough at the time. She supposed when she spoke to a neurologist she could voice some of her concerns – but who knew how long that would be. Perhaps she would just get better and forget all these worries; she could only hope.

"You dad will be pleased to see you," Mum said, Macy smiled, but kept her eyes closed. That made her feel a little less ill. "How is the pain today?"

"Still there. Always there. But manageable, I suppose." She didn't like how direct she was being; she was sure that before she would have cushioned such comments; not been so blunt with someone who cared about her so much. But she found that even that required too much energy: she could give the facts, but nothing more.

The countryside whizzed past them and when Macy opened her eyes they were reaching the familiar wilderness of the borders. Inhabitants between England and Scotland were not plentiful and along the road she spotted an occasional farmhouse or factory, but there were few large towns or dwellings. The village she had grown up in was tiny: a handful of houses, and probably the same amount of farms, surrounded by fields. The nearest town was twenty minutes away and even that was tiny – well, compared to living in a city, anyway. She had grown bored of living somewhere so rural long before she was old enough to leave. She had learnt to drive the second she turned seventeen, having her first driving lesson on her seventeenth birthday, because she needed to feel like she could get out. And then at eighteen she had left, gone to university in Newcastle and not looked back.

Until now.

Twelve years later, and she had lived in the city ever since – enjoying visits to see her parents, but preferring when they came to visit her. Never had she considered moving back home.

Until now.

But it wasn't permanent, she told herself. A few weeks of recuperation; the neurologist had seemed confident that she would be back to normal at some point. She was only thirty – even thinking that felt odd – so surely her body could recover from this. Surely her mind could recover from this.

"I don't understand why this has happened," Macy said suddenly.

"Me neither."

"It doesn't seem fair."

"It's not. But I'm grateful you're still here, and able to walk, and talk…"

"I know. And I'm grateful for those things too but…" She paused while she tried to think how to put into words what she wanted to say. It was hard to know whether thinking of the words was harder because of the stroke, or because what she wanted to say was hard.

"I'm also really angry. I don't want to be grateful; this shouldn't have happened. And now I'm scared every time something hurts that I'm about to drop down dead, or become paralysed, or lose the ability to speak… I don't want to be terrified or ill for the rest of my life. I don't want to be on medication for the rest of my life. It's – hopefully – a long time to put up with all that."

Macy glanced at her mum and saw she was crying, and instantly felt bad for her outburst.

"I'm sorry, Mum," she said.

"Don't be sorry," Mum said, her voice thick with tears. "You're right. I just... I hate thinking how close we were to losing you. I hate thinking that the world is so unpredictable, that you can live a normal life and still end up with something like this happening. So I'm trying to see some good... With difficulty."

"I know you are," Macy said, not saying what she was thinking now: that she did not want to think positively. That she wanted to be angry and rail against everything that had happened to her, at least for a bit. Perhaps feeling grateful and positive would help down the line – but for now, it wasn't helping anything.

"We'll look after you, until you're better. And then this will just be a blip that you can look back on in years to come and think '*thank God I got through that.*'"

◆ ◆ ◆

Macy spent three days in bed after that car journey. It just seemed to wipe her out; but she found she didn't really have the will to get up and do anything either. She didn't feel well enough - so what was the point? So she spent her days lying in the small double bed that she had crammed into her room when she was a teenager, and watching shows on her laptop - because the pink TV in her room from the days when she had lived there was no longer really good enough to watch anything on. Her eyes were already fuzzy; she didn't need a poor TV picture on top of that.

Her parents cam in regularly to check on her, although Dad was at work at his garage most days, so in the day it was just Mum. But in the evenings, Dad would come and sit on the wooden chair in the corner of her room, and try to make conversation.

Macy had always tried to make conversation easier, with whomever she was conversing with - but right now, she didn't have the energy for that.

"The weather's improving," he said on the third evening, as Macy drank her hundredth cup of tea that day, propped up in bed with pink pillows that she now despised.

"That's good."

"I saw Miss Mason - do you remember, she taught you in Year Six? She came in with a flat tyre today. Asked about you."

"What did you tell her?" Macy asked.

"Told her about your job in the city, but how you've not been well, so you're home with us for a bit."

Macy hated how much she cringed inside, thinking of everyone knowing she had moved back home. She had always prided herself on being independent - hell, it was part of her personality. And yet now...

Now she realised that she had nobody, aside from her parents.

And she loved them so much, and everything they had done for her...

But shouldn't she have someone else, by now?

A support system? People she could rely on to look after her - and not have to move back to her childhood bedroom because she'd had a stupid stroke before she had even turned thirty years old?

There was no point in obsessing over what was missing in her life, she knew; and yet she found herself doing it anyway.

If she had died when the stroke had happened... what would she have achieved? How would her life have been summarised? Who would even have come to her funeral?

She couldn't share such morbid thoughts, but they were there in her head - and they were making it difficult to have conversations with her dad about the weather.

"Your mum's making bolognese for dinner," he said.

"That'll be nice."

\*   \*   \*

"I'm going to to go for a walk," Mum said, a day or two later. Macy found the days were melding into one - she wasn't even sure what day of the week it was any more, let alone the date. "Do you want to come with me?"

"I don't think…"

"I think you need to get out. We won't go far - just a bit of fresh air."

"I'm just worried…"

"I know. But the doctors didn't say you needed to stay in bed all the time - and I don't think it's doing you any good, mentally."

Macy nodded; she knew her mum was right, even if she didn't want to accept it.

"Get dressed - we'll just have wander round the footpath, okay?"

"Okay Mum," Macy said.

She dragged herself out of bed, letting her feet rest on the rug for a moment. She hadn't got properly dressed in a couple of days, but thankfully she had an easy pair of jogging bottoms and a hoodie that she could throw on with minimal effort. When she tried to tighten the string on the bottoms, however, she found her hand slipped, and she became frustrated. She had noticed - although pretended not to - that she was struggling with delicate tasks a little. Pouring hot water into a cup of tea; putting her hair up; buttoning her pyjama top. It wasn't impossible, but it was definitely more difficult.

And that was something she hoped was not going to be permanent.

By the time she was wearing enough to be warm and decent on their walk, she was out of breath, and swearing in her head.

"All right?"

She nodded, even though it was a lie, and sat at the kitchen table to pull her boots on. Misty, her parents ancient cat, rubbed herself against Macy's legs before disappearing in search of food.

"I haven't got any energy," Macy warned her mum.

"I know," Mum said. "Just a little walk."

Macy nodded, and pulled herself to her feet, following Mum out the door.

The sky was blue and the air crisp, and Macy was pleased she had grabbed her coat on the way out of the house. Spring hadn't quite sprung, but it was clearly on its way; Macy just wished she was feeling the hope of the season as she normally did.

The house was surrounded by farms, but many

had public footpaths through them, and so Mum opened a gate and carefully closed it behind them. The ground was fairly solid, thanks to a lack of rain lately, and the field empty of inhabitants, so they could walk at leisure without being disturbed.

The brown fields stretched on for miles; some had livestock, some empty, one had a tractor moving through it. Macy had always liked the fields, but her favourite part of home was being near the sea; she would have to make it to the beach soon, she thought.

"Have you heard from the doctors?" Mum asked, although Macy would have told her if she had.

Macy shook her head.

"You need to chase them up… they need to do tests, see if they need you on these high dose medications…"

"I feel about a hundred," Macy said.

"I know. It won't last forever…"

More positivity; but Macy couldn't feel positive right now.

Her heart suddenly felt like it was accelerating, and she paused and leaned on a fence post, taking deep breaths of the cool air.

"Are you okay?"

She shook her head again. "My heart…"

"I think it's anxiety," Mum said, although she didn't look completely confident.

"Maybe…"

"They didn't see anything wrong with your heart on the ECG, love," she reminded her.

"They didn't see me having a stroke in A and E," Macy snapped back.

"I know…" Mum said, and Macy felt bad for her reaction.

"Sorry."

"It's fine. You're bound to be anxious. Maybe you need to speak to someone…"

"I don't need to be put on more medication for my anxiety," Macy said, trying hard to keep breathing and not panic. "I just don't want to be scared every time anything hurts…"

Mum squeezed her arm. "You won't. It's early days - this will pass."

"When?" she asked, tears in her eyes.

"Soon, I'm sure. You've done amazingly to come out for a walk. Maybe tomorrow you could come to the supermarket with me?"

Macy nodded. "Maybe. Can we go home, now?"

"Of course," Mum said. "There's a stile up ahead, anyway - not sure that's the best plan right now!"

Macy laughed, because she was right; with her co-ordination the way it was, it was likely to be a disaster.

"Maybe next week," she said, and Mum smiled.

\* \* \*

Macy stared at herself in the mirror the next morning. The image was still a bit blurry - the issues with her eyes hadn't settled down yet - and she was pretty sure she had lost weight. Her face was pale, and her hair was getting knotted through a total lack of care.

It wasn't helping, she realised. The anxiety was overwhelming, the pains everywhere debilitating, the exhaustion crippling.

But she couldn't hide away in bed forever.

"Mum," she shouted, as she exited her bedroom, to find Mum sat on the sofa with a cup of a tea and a magazine. "I will come with you to the supermarket, later."

Mum's face lit up. "That's great. We can get a drink and a cake at the cafe, too, if you like."

Macy smiled; it reminded her of being a kid, and the sneaky treats she and Mum used to have when they went to do the weekly food shop.

"I thought I might have a bath, first…"

"I'll run it for you," Mum said, immediately putting her cup down on the coffee table.

"Thanks, Mum," Macy said. "I'm not going to lock the door… just in case…"

Mum nodded; "You'll be fine. But shout, if you need anything."

Macy nodded. Hopefully once her hair was clean and less knotty, and she was wearing proper clothes, she might feel a little more like herself. She felt like she was in mourning for life before all this had happened - but now she really wanted to try to move past it.

❖ ❖ ❖

It was a ten minute drive to the nearest supermarket, through narrow winding country lanes. Dad had taken their car to work, so Mum drove Macy's, since she still wasn't cleared to drive yet.

"I'll ring the doctors tomorrow," Macy said as they drove. "Find out where we go next."

"That sounds like a good plan," Mum said. "I can drive you back if you need to go for appointments."

Macy smiled. "It's like being a teenager again -

waiting for you to give me lifts."

"I hate the circumstances," Mum said. "But it's nice having you home."

The supermarket was fairly busy, and Macy chose to push the trolley, leaning most of her weight on it as they perused the aisles. She didn't have much of an appetite still, but Mum's cooking was always good. It was something she had missed, moving away from home, and it was a bonus to being back.

"We need to grab some more paracetamol," Mum said, as they entered the medicine aisle. "And ibuprofen for Dad - I know you can't take it with your medicines."

"Macy? Macy Maxwell?"

Macy turned at the sound of her name, and then froze. Six foot three, blonde hair and piercing blue eyes: Joe Kriss had been the subject of many of her fantasies throughout secondary school. In fact, the crush had started even before then, she thought. Nothing had ever happened between them, but she had imagined them dating for years and years.

He was just as gorgeous - no, more gorgeous - as he was back then, she thought. Now he had a bit of stubble, and muscles, and somehow looked even taller.

"Joe! Hi."

"Long time no see! I didn't think you lived around here anymore."

"I don't," Macy said, as Mum wandered off to find what they needed.

"Oh," Joe said.

"Do you?"

He nodded; "I've got a scaffolding firm, over in Alnwick," he said. "So not far. Just spending the day with my parents. Where are you living now?"

"Newcastle," she said, aware that her eye was starting to twitch. It had been doing it off and on since the stroke, but now she hoped it wasn't noticeable. "I'm... I've not been well, so I'm recuperating with my parents for a bit."

"Oh. Sorry to hear that…"

Was he imagining all the gruesome things that could be wrong with her in his beautiful head? Was that worse than knowing the truth?

"I had a stroke," she said suddenly, and then regretted it. Shock and pity filled her eyes, and he tilted his head to once side.

"That's awful. Are you… okay?"

"I will be," she said.

"We'll have to catch up, if you're around for a

while," he said.

She nodded, although it sounded like a rather awkward idea.

"Lisa - my wife - would love to have you round for dinner."

Wow. That sounded even more awkward.

Wife?

She hadn't even known he was married. He didn't seem to have a social media presence, and well, asking her parents if they knew what he was doing had always seemed a bit stalker-ish. Especially since they had never actually even dated - not outside of her dreams.

"Lovely," she said, a fake smile plastered on her face.

"Hope you feel better soon", he said, walking away.

"And you," Macy said, then realised the stupid words that had exited her mouth and wanted the ground to open up and swallow her.

So her crush was married, with a business.

And she was living at home with a brain that didn't want to work properly.

Marvellous.

# CHAPTER FOUR

"That neurologist is ringing me today," Macy said, as she sat and ate a piece of toast with Mum at the table. She wasn't really sure what Mum had done with her days before all this. She didn't want to stop her living her life, but, at the same time, she didn't really want to be left alone.

"That's good. Have you written down your list of questions?"

Macy nodded. "Yeah. I'll try to get some answers…"

"I was going to see Lara this afternoon - do you want to come?"

Macy shook her head; she wasn't feeling up to socialising with anyone, let alone one of her mother's oldest friends. "Sorry. Don't feel up to it."

"That's fine," Mum said, taking a bite of toast. "I'll wait till your dad gets home, and go. He finishes early today."

"You don't have to…" Macy started to say, then paused; she really didn't want to be alone. "Thanks, Mum," she finished.

"No problem," Mum said with a smile. "I've been doing some research... and I've found a group."

"What sort of group?"

"A support group... for people who have had strokes. I got in touch with the woman who runs it - she works for a charity - and she said there are a couple of younger people there, so you wouldn't be the only one."

"I'm not sure..." Macy said, sipping her tea and realising it had already gone cold. "I don't know if..."

"See if the neurologist has any answers," Mum said. "But I think it might do you good, to speak with people who get what you're going through. You've got to deal with this terrible thing that has happened to you, and I'm not sure how much help I am."

"You're so helpful," Macy said, knowing that there was no way she would have got through all this without Mrs Donna Maxwell.

"Even so," Mum said, "There's people out there who will understand all this far more than me. Just promise me you'll think about it, all right?"

"I will."

❖ ❖ ❖

"Can I speak to Miss Macy Maxwell, please?"

"Speaking."

"Excellent. This is Dr Histon, the neurologist. I wanted to discuss the plan we have, for investigating your stroke. How are you feeling?"

"Not great," Macy admitted. "Everything aches, my head still hurts, I still feel dizzy…"

The doctor made sympathetic noises over the phone.

"Is there any way we can reduce these statins? I feel like my whole body is ancient."

She could hear papers being shuffled in the background. "The truth is, Miss Maxwell, we still don't know why you had the stroke. And therefore we need to prevent another happening - and the blood thinners, and the high dose of statins, is our best way of doing that. I could lower the dose… but there would be some risk involved."

"I don't want to take any risks," Macy said, feeling panic beginning to rise up in her. "I… feel so anxious, all the time, about it happening again."

"It's unlikely to now, Miss Maxwell - we have you on the right medications, and it's been nearly two weeks since the stroke happened. But we need to figure out what's going on. So, I'd like you to go for a more in depth scan of your heart - and we're going to send you a machine, to monitor your heart rhythms for a longer period. And I'd like to schedule another scan, to look at your neck…"

"I thought they'd done that?" Macy asked. "To look for some kind of torn artery?"

"The pictures aren't as clear as we'd like, and with your age… well, we want to make sure. And we're still waiting on your blood results, just to rule out any disorders."

"Okay," Macy said, feeling like her head was spinning with too much information.

"And you can speak to your GP, if the anxiety gets too much…"

Macy nodded, and then realised that the doctor could not see her. "Okay."

"It really is totally normal," the doctor said. "The anxiety, the fatigue, the fear… for the first few months after a stroke. It will settle down."

"I hope so."

"I'm confident it will."

Macy ended the call by giving her parents' address for any correspondence. It was no good pretending she was leaving any time soon: she still didn't feel well enough to be left alone in the house, let alone going days without seeing anyone like she would at home. Work had the 12-week sick note, so she was not in any rush; and as much as moving home had felt like going backwards, she didn't particularly relish the thought of going forwards by herself at the minute, either.

Maybe she should speak to a GP. Her heart kept racing lately, whenever she exerted herself even slightly, but she kept trying to convince herself it was just anxiety. She went to bed wondering whether she would wake up, and woke up wondering whether the day would be filled with pain and sickness.

Or maybe this group that Mum had mentioned could help. After all, people who understood these feelings... they might make her feel better. And if at least a couple of people were a similar age, maybe she could see how they had moved past it, and lived full lives: not spent the rest of their days worrying about dying, as she thought she was at risk of doing.

Maybe they could give her an idea of how long it would take to get better, to feel like herself again, to not be too scared to lock a door or be out of her parents' sight.

Or maybe nobody had those answers.

◆ ◆ ◆

The TV was on in the background, but Macy didn't think any of them were really listening. Macy was staring into space, mulling over the path her life had taken; Mum was scrolling on her phone; Dad was doing invoices on his laptop. Applause rang out from the quiz show, and Macy glanced at it, before looking back at the spot on the ceiling she had been focussing on. She fiddled with her fingers, and tried to stop herself tearing off a nail that had caught.

Time seemed to be passing slowly; and yet somehow it had been three weeks since she had had the stroke.

Three weeks.

Stroke.

It still didn't quite feel real.

Everyone told her to take the time she needed to heal - but she wanted to be well already. She wanted to be able to drive, to be able to paint, to be at work complaining about how far it seemed to be until the weekend finally arrived. To be planning her next night out, not wondering when the neurologist would be calling. To be taking painkillers for a hangover, instead of a handful of tablets that felt like they were the only thing between her and another stroke that might finish her off - or worse.

That terrified her too, perhaps even more than the thought of dying: the idea of waking up paralysed, or unable to speak, or both.

"When's that group, Mum?" she asked, more to change the direction of her thoughts than anything else. She saw Mum smile at Dad, and wondered how many nights they spent, once she had gone to bed, discussing her. Discussing how little progress she was making, probably; or how miserable she seemed.

"Friday," Mum said. "It's at the Old Duck, over in Berwick. I can drop you in."

"Maybe," Macy said, unwilling to commit, even though she had brought it up. "Why's it in a pub? I don't think getting wasted is going to solve any of my problems."

Mum laughed awkwardly. "It's in the morning… I would guess it's just a place that has space of a morning, and probably welcomes the custom - even if it is all lemonades and waters."

"I guess," Macy said, grabbing a magazine from the coffee table.

❖ ❖ ❖

She did go, in the end, because she couldn't think of a reason not to.

And she hoped, deep down, that it might help.

Mum dropped her off outside the pub.

"Just ring whenever you're ready," she said, with

a smile, and Macy tried to smile back. She was nervous: nervous about meeting new people, and nervous about being out on her own.

She watched Mum drive away, and took several long, deep breaths. There was nothing to be worried about; if she hated it, she didn't have to return.

She tried the door to the pub, and found it locked. Then she noticed the sign on the door; it didn't open for another hour.

Did she have the wrong location?

Panic set in again - she was alone and in the wrong place it seemed, and Mum had gone home.

Maybe there was another entrance. She wandered around the back, knowing she must look very odd, lurking around a pub at ten in the morning when it hadn't even opened, and then felt an overwhelming sense of relief at the sight of a beer garden with a back door open.

Heart beating, she made her way through it, and a woman behind the bar glanced up at her.

"We're not open yet," she said, not stopping in her drying of a glass.

"I'm looking for the stroke group?" Macy said, almost like a question, and she was sure the woman looked her up and down before jerking her head backwards. "Round the corner. Do you want a drink?"

"Lemonade, please," she said, grabbing some change to pay for it before following the sound of voices around the corner she had pointed to.

There were about ten people there, sat at tables, chatting away animatedly, although she couldn't hear the topic. A dark-haired young woman waved.

"Macy, is it?" she asked. "I'm Lexi - I spoke to your mum, I think."

Macy nodded, feeling shy, as well as embarrassed that she was the thirty-year-old whose mum was making phone calls for her.

"Come, come, sit down," she said. "Take a seat next to Levi, here."

"Thanks," she said, shuffling into the seat indicated and sitting down more heavily than she had intended.

"Hi, Macy is it?" the man next to her asked. He was about sixty, she would have guessed. He smiled at her, and she smiled back.

"Yeah," she said.

"I'm Levi. Nice to meet you."

"And you."

"You had a stroke about a month ago, is that right, Macy?" Lexi asked, and Macy found herself counting backwards in her head to try to remember.

"Yeah… four weeks tomorrow," she said.

"You're so young!" a woman on the other side of the table cried.

"Thirty," Macy said, with a sad smile.

"Crazy."

"Poor love."

"How are you doing?" a man in a wheelchair asked her, and suddenly she seemed to be on the spot, everyone listening to what she had to say.

"I… My vision isn't great," she said, honestly. "And my head hurts. And I'm so tired…"

"Tell me about it," a woman in red stilettos in the corner said to her. "I'm a year on and still get exhausted."

"I'm at ten years!" another said. "And still sometimes get to that point where I can't go on."

"So it's normal?" Macy asked.

"Totally. It will get better, with time," Levi said with a smile.

"And what about being constantly terrified you're

going to die?" she asked, voicing her darkest thoughts.

"That gets better too," Levi said, softly.

"And then you get to my age, and you worry all over again," a man with a wheeze said.

"Shut up, Jack," someone else said, and they all laughed.

At the minute she wondered if she would ever reach whatever advanced age he was - but she didn't say that.

"Do they know what caused it yet?" Jack asked.

Macy shook her head.

"Get them to investigate an artery tear," someone said. "Always the way with young people and strokes it seems!"

"Or a hole in the heart!" another voice piped up.

A conversation ensued that Macy had never imagined being a part of: the listing of types of strokes, and the reasons for them. She sat and sipped her lemonade, and mostly listened, for although so many of the people here were much older than her, they gave her hope; and made her feel much more normal.

"Sorry I'm late." A man more her own age walked over, helped on one side with a crutch. He had jet black hair and green eyes, and Macy found she was instantly interested in knowing more about him. More interested than she had been in anything lately.

"Bus was late," he said, rolling his eyes.

"No problem," Lexi said. "Come and sit - this is Macy, it's her first time here. Macy, this is Sam."

"Hi," she said, with a smile, and found herself wondering if her hair was still as wild as it had been this morning. Had she dealt with it, before she came out? She couldn't remember.

"Hi. Sorry to see you here!" he said, and then laughed. It took her a moment to get what he meant, but she smiled.

"It's not the greatest club to be a part of," he said, putting his bag down. "Although the people are the greatest!"

There were cheers of agreement, and Macy laughed.

"What are you in for?"

"Cerebellar stroke," she said. "Last month. You?"

"Frontal lobe stroke," he said. "Two years ago. Left side of the brain - it's why I need this to help me get around," he said, waving the crutch he still held in his right hand. "Cerebellar strokes… they're quite rare, aren't they?"

"I think so," she said. "They sent me home and said it was a migraine."

He rolled his eyes; "They never suspect a stroke when you're young. I had slurred speech and couldn't walk, and they thought I was drunk for hours, even though I hadn't touched a drink, just because I was young."

"How young?" Macy asked. She had a thirst for knowledge about strokes, and especially young strokes, and especially, she thought, anything to do with his stroke.

"Thirty-two," he said. "How about you?"

"Twenty-nine," she said. "The day before my thirtieth birthday."

He let out a low whistle. "What a crappy way to celebrate your birthday."

"Tell me about it!"

"So, do you live round here?"

"I… I grew up near here," she said. "I live in Newcastle, normally. But I've moved back with my parents, while I recuperate."

He nodded; "Sounds like a sensible plan. Don't want to be alone and worried all the time."

"Exactly."

"My mum's only just let me move out," he said with a laugh. "Again, I mean. I lived on my own, then after the stroke moved back in with them. But moving back to a flat up three flights of stairs wasn't exactly ideal when my right side doesn't like to co-operate." He laughed, but she was sure she could see pain in his eyes. She felt a wave of gratitude that she didn't have any loss of motion from her stroke; it was rubbish, but it could have been so much worse.

"But I've found a ground floor place now, and persuaded her I can cope on my own. Wouldn't think I was going to be thirty-five this year!"

Macy laughed; "I think they'll always worry."

"Probably. Maybe when - if - I have kids, I'll feel the same."

"Maybe," Macy said, and then the conversation around them took over, and she let herself zone out for a minute. She felt like her whole body was fragile now, just waiting for something to be too much. Were children even on the table for her any more? Not that she had a partner with which to have children, but still... she had always thought she had the option.

Something else, she supposed, to chat with the neurologist about.

"So," Lexi was saying, as Macy refocussed. "The

next outing is bowling, in Edinburgh - next Friday. The bus will pick us up, so I'll just need numbers. And then next month we're thinking Bamburgh beach - yes, it will be chilly, but you lot voted for it. Fish and chips by the sea, and a wander for those who feel up to it - we could do a castle tour, if you like."

"Are you coming?" Sam asked her. "It's usually a laugh, and there's another lad, Jamie - he's a similar age to us too. He often comes along."

"Maybe," she said. "I've not been feeling up to much…"

He nodded; "I get it. The fatigue is overwhelming sometimes."

"I'm so dizzy still, so often."

"But if you feel up to it…"

"I'll try. I don't want to just give in to it all…"

"It's not been long," he said. "Try to give yourself some time! It's a major thing."

"I guess. I just…" She felt silly, spilling her guts to a virtual stranger, but his green eyes and easy smile seemed to be willing her to continue.

"I keep expecting myself to be better than I am. Because I didn't even know I'd had a stroke for a week…"

"Doesn't change the fact that you did have one," he said with a shrug. "Try not to dwell on it - it doesn't help to."

"I guess. I just sit at home with my parents all the time."

"I remember that. Maybe see if your friends can come to you, if you don't feel up to going out?"

"What friends?" she said with a laugh, and then realised how sad that sounded. "I mean… they've not really been in touch, to be honest, since the stroke."

He made an irritated tutting sound. "Oh, I remember that too. It's amazing how many people are available to go out drinking, or to go on holiday, but when you nearly die they can barely manage to send a text asking if you're still alive."

"Exactly!" she said, feeling understood at last. "Exactly."

"I'm sorry. People are shit. I had the same. But you'll make new friends - better friends."

"Yeah, I guess - if I ever leave my parents' living room."

"You will," he said, with a grin. "Now, I would get you a drink, but I can't carry two back here."

"Oh, I'll get it," she said, feeling rude for not having

suggested it already. "What would you like?"

◆ ◆ ◆

When she text her mum to ask for a lift home, her soul was feeling a little lighter. She had agreed to come back to the next meeting in a fortnight, and had been added to the large group chat that they had going. She was even considering going to one of the next outings - although she thought she'd better wait and see how exhausted she was after this experience first.

"How was it?" Mum asked eagerly, as soon as Macy got in the car.

"It was... good," Macy said, with a smile. "I think I'll go again."

"Were they nice? Anyone your age?"

Macy answered her questions as best she could, and tried to accept that she would need a lie down after so much socialising. It was part of life now that she had to accept, she supposed - for however long it lasted.

"I'm shattered," she said, when they got home.

"I bet you are."

"Mind if I go and lie down?"

"Course not - I'll make some lunch, but if you're asleep, I'll just keep it 'til later."

"Thanks Mum."

She slipped off her shoes and lay down on top of the duvet. Her head hurt, her whole body was tired, but she needed a moment before she tried to sleep.

Instead she scrolled through the messages on her phone. It had been days since anyone had messaged her. She was with Mum and Dad all the time, and none of her friends seemed to have thought to do so.

She'd had some, at the beginning, when she'd messaged to say what had happened to her, and that she was going to stay with her parents. They had sounded sympathetic and now, a month later…

They'd vanished.

She needed to accept that, and move on. There seemed to be so much she needed to move on from after the disaster that had struck her. The issues with her physical capabilities, and her mental ones too. Wondering if she would ever be back to normal again. Wondering if the life she had envisioned would ever actually be a reality.

And accepting that the people she had thought were friends were fair-weather friends at best. Sam had been right, presumably from experience: they were there when a night out was to be had, but not when the going got tough.

And boy, had the going got tough.

How had she reached thirty years old without having anyone she could rely on, except the people who had brought her into this world? The thought made her angry and frustrated, and she closed her messages and flicked through social media instead.

Engagement pictures. Pregnancy announcement. Pictures of keys in front of brand new front doors. Photos of babies and puppies and kittens and all sorts of life events that Macy could barely think about right now.

She dropped her phone on the floor and cursed loudly.

"Macy?" Mum said, bursting through the door. "Sorry, I thought… I was worried you'd fallen."

Macy tried to smile. "Sorry. No… just had enough."

"Of anything in particular?"

"Life?" Macy suggested, but then winced at the sad look in her Mum's eyes. "No, it's just… I thought I had good friends. But they've all disappeared, now that I'm ill."

Mum sat on the edge of the bed. "Some friends are just there for certain periods of your life, love. There'll be other friends - better ones, I'm sure."

"I hope so."

"You want some lunch?"

"I just want to sleep," Macy said, feeling like even talking was too much work.

"You sleep. Don't stress about anyone - just focus on getting better, okay? They're not worth it."

REBECCA PAULINYI

# CHAPTER FIVE

It was the longest she had ever been home and not been to the beach. It was one of the greatest things about living in this part of the world, she thought; the proximity to so many beautiful beaches. The weather was never particularly warm, and she knew that down south the beaches were busier, probably due to the better weather – but she thought nothing rivalled Northumberland for beautiful coastline.

She wouldn't have minded going alone; it had been a long time now since she had spent any time alone, and although it was nice to feel safe, she was used to more solo time. However, she still hadn't been cleared to drive, and anyway, she wasn't sure she felt well enough to be totally alone yet.

Thankfully, Mum was up for a very slow walk on the beach, and they drove to Spittal, where the sky was a darker navy than the sea. There was a decent chance of rain, but Macy knew she wouldn't be up for walking for long anyway.

"I'm just gonna go down to the water, for a minute," Macy said, hoping Mum understood she needed a minute to herself.

Mum nodded, and took longer than was probably necessary to lock the car and put on her coat.

Macy picked her way down the wet sand until she was near to where the waves crashed into the beach. She didn't really want to get wet feet, so she did not go too close; for a while she simply watched them going in and out, crashing at different points and dragging out whatever sound they could, before dumping it back again on the next round. She felt a bit like she was being buffeted by those seas at the minute, in her life. This stroke had been so unexpected, and now seemed to leave her with so much to deal with. The realisation her friends were not all she had thought they were; and that perhaps her job was not making her as happy as she had thought it was.

Everything she had expected from life... Was it even possible now? Were marriage and children and buying a house on the horizon, as she had always thought they were? Or would she spend years living with her parents, getting back onto her feet, before realising that the best years of her life were gone? Was it already too late?

Thoughts buzzed in her head like a swarm of bees, refusing to let up. She tried to breathe in time with the crashing waves, to calm herself down – but instead more worries just seem to add to the pile.

What if she had another stroke? What if this one finished her off, or left her unable to look after herself? What if she was given this second chance, and still made a mess of it?

The crunching of mum's feet on the wet sand was the only thing that broke her from her troubled reverie. Mum stood beside her and for a moment they didn't speak, just soaked up the wild atmosphere of the empty beach.

"Are you okay?"

"No," Macy said, truthfully.

"Can I help?"

Tears filled Macy's eyes as she shook her head. "I wish you could. I don't know what will help…"

"Things will get better Macy, I really believe it. I know it all seems dark now…"

Macy nodded. She had heard all this before, but for some reason, right now it wasn't helping. Perhaps what she needed to do right now was wallow, grieve for the life that she'd had before the stroke, a life that seemed so far away now.

"You could talk to someone. A professional, maybe. I just wish I could help you…"

"Maybe," Macy said, staring at the hazy point where the sea met the sky. "Maybe."

◆ ◆ ◆

They didn't talk much on the way home, and sat at the kitchen table and ate lunch in silence. Macy just couldn't snap herself out of the mood she was in. On top of the aches and pains that plagued her daily, she couldn't shake the feeling that everything might not work out all right. That maybe she'd had her chance at life, and not done a great job at it.

A knock at the door interrupted their awkward silence, and Mum jumped up to answer it. Macy tried to muster up some interest in who was calling round, but it wasn't until two more people walked into the living room that she actually paid any attention.

"Marion's popped over for a cup of tea," Mum said, looking almost a little hesitant to share this information. "And she's brought Hayley. Isn't that nice?"

"Lovely," said Macy, feeling like it was anything but. She and Hayley had been good friends in primary school – probably because their mums were good friends – and even through most of secondary school, but had lost touch in later years. Macy barely had the energy to make conversation with her own mother, let alone anybody else – but now they were here, there wasn't much that could be done about it. She wondered if mum had arranged this, or whether it really was just a surprise visit.

"We heard you'd been really ill, Macy," Marion said, putting her handbag down on the table and sitting down, as mum went to put the kettle on.

Macy nodded. What else was there to do?

"A stroke, at your age – it's unbelievable. You poor thing."

Macy found she had nothing to say to that, either. She had never noticed how much energy conversing took up – especially when it was with people whom you didn't speak with regularly, or perhaps doesn't want to speak to.

"Are you feeling any better now?" Hayley asked. Macy thoughts that she didn't really look any different from when they were in secondary school. Hadn't changed; hadn't aged.

"A bit, thanks," Macy said. They didn't really want to know. If she listed all her daily aches, pains, vision issues, and other nightmares to them, she knew the room would be filled with an awkward silence. But she couldn't bring herself to lie, and say everything was all right. Because it really wasn't.

"That's good. And you've been so lucky; it could have been so much worse."

Anger boiled up inside Macy, and she tried desperately to tamp it back down. Wasn't that true about everyone's lives, all the time? Couldn't it always be worse? She wasn't sure that was a useful way of looking at problems in life. It certainly didn't make her feel any better.

"I don't feel that lucky..." She said, feeling like something needed to be said, but not wishing to be as rude as she was being in her head.

"Of – of course not," Hayley said, stumbling over her words at Macy's frank tone. "I just mean... At least you aren't paralysed."

"Or dead," Macy said, without any hint of emotion.

Mum walked back in with a tray of tea at that point, and looked embarrassed.

"You're getting there, slowly, aren't you love," Mum said, and Macy allowed her to smooth over everything – although she didn't take part in the rest of the conversation very much. Yes, of course she was lucky that she was alive, and had use of her legs, and her voice... But what would have been luckier was to not have had a stroke at the age of twenty-nine. It was tempting to tell them that they were lucky to be eating the biscuits in front of them, because plenty of people didn't have biscuits, or were diabetic; that they were lucky to be in a warm house and not outside in the rain, because plenty of people were homeless, or had inadequate shelter. Somehow people seemed to think that when something terrible happened it was helpful to look at how lucky you had been. And maybe, in time, that would be true. But at that moment, Macy felt it was supremely unhelpful. It would have been better for them to simply say how terrible it was… Perhaps offer some help, perhaps ask about her experience. But if anyone else told her she was lucky, she was worried she might not be so polite.

When they left, she felt like Mum might want to talk to her about the conversation, or maybe chastise her for being rude. She couldn't face any of that. So she went to bed, despite the fact that it was only early evening, and pulled the covers over her head and pretended the world outside didn't exist. Just her in the dark and warmth of the duvet fort. No other people; no strokes; no upcoming hospital appointments – just her, and sleep.

When it came, it was filled with unpleasant dreams that bordered on nightmares – but it carried her right through till morning.

# CHAPTER SIX

It had been five days since Macy had properly got dressed. Instead she had sat around the house in pyjamas, watching box sets of old comedy shows with cringy laughter tracks, and eating chocolate. She didn't have the energy or the inclination to do anything else - so she didn't.

She wasn't so scared of being alone any more, so when Mum said she needed to go to the supermarket, Macy suggested she go alone. Every pain in her head still made her wonder if she was having a stroke, but if that was going to happen, then it was going to happen. There wasn't much anyone could do for her if it *did* happen - so Mum being at the shops wouldn't make much difference. After all, when she had gone to the one place she should have been safe, they hadn't even picked up that she was having a stroke. Hell, the nurse hadn't even believed she was ill enough to need the wheelchair. So her confidence in their magical life-saving abilities was certainly diminished.

Three days after the beach trip, Macy was reminded of the stroke group outing - bowling in

Edinburgh.

She made her excuses, feeling like a whole afternoon out was more than her mind or body could take, and spent the rest of that day watching a film that made her cry. Well, better to cry over pretend misery than her own, she thought.

Several members of the chat said they hoped to see her at the next outing, to Bamburgh beach. She hadn't been there in years, but she had always loved it - yet she doubted she would feel up to the social aspect by the time the trip came round, let alone the physical challenge.

"How's your eye sight?" Dad asked that evening, as they watched a game show on the television.

"Still fuzzy," she said, with a sigh. "I'm almost getting used to it."

"Maybe you should get your eyes checked. See if there's anything they can do to help. It would be nice to get your driving licence back."

She supposed it would be, although whether she would ever have the confidence to drive again, without worrying something terrible was going to happen while she was behind the wheel, she didn't know. Now that she had passed a month post-stroke without recurrence, her vision was the only obstacle to being allowed to drive.

"I can book you an appointment," Mum said, from

the armchair in the corner.

"Yeah, maybe," Macy said. She felt like that was her attitude to everything at the minute. Struggling to commit, but with no energy to change her perspective. Everything just felt so hard...

◆ ◆ ◆

She didn't make her mind up until the morning of the trip, when she decided that another day indoors was not going to do her any good. She needed a break from all the thinking and dwelling, and she needed to see other people, other places.

At nine o'clock she text the group chat, letting them know she would meet them in time for the bus.

By half past nine, she was dressed and had organised for Mum to give her a lift into town, where the minibus would be collecting them all. Apparently they used it regularly, for it needed to fit several people in wheelchairs, and most of group members didn't drive either. The day wasn't particularly warm, but it wasn't raining either - and that was always a bonus in the borders between England and Scotland.

"You've got enough layers?" Mum asked, and Macy nodded. "And a coat?" It was a cardinal rule of living so far North: never go out without some sort of rain coat.

"Yes Mum," she said, and laughed. "It reminds me of when I used to go on school trips."

Mum grinned. "Me too."

"And you've made me a packed lunch!"

"Don't want you to be hungry!"

"We'll probably get chips or something," Macy said.

"But just in case…"

"Thanks Mum."

"I think this is a good idea. I don't like to see you so cooped up at home."

Macy nodded. It was really hard to talk about how she felt, but she hoped that this would indeed help her to feel a bit better.

"I'll be here at three, unless you message, okay?"

Macy nodded again. "Sorry you have to run around after me."

"I don't mind," Mum said. "I wish you weren't ill, but it's nice having you home for a bit!"

Macy couldn't help but hope that it wouldn't become a long-term situation, but she didn't say that. Instead she took her bag - and old rucksack, with her lunch, coat and purse in - and made her way to the meeting point.

The minibus had just arrived, and they were getting everyone to board, starting with those with wheelchairs. There was lots of waving and hellos, and Macy noticed herself smiling when she noticed Sam stood at the front of the line to get on.

"Macy!"

"So glad you could make it!"

"How are you feeling?"

By the time she was on the bus, she had been greeted by most of the group, and even introduced to a couple of the members who hadn't been there when she had attended. The bus was pretty full, but there was a seat spare next to Sam, and he waved her over.

She didn't think twice about taking it.

"We missed you at bowling!" he said.

She smiled. "Maybe next time."

"How are things going?"

She shrugged.

"Fed up of being asked that?"

"I just don't really know how to answer. I'm not sure how honest people want me to be…"

"You can be honest with me," he said. "But I know what you mean. You start to wonder if people just want you to nod and say you're fine."

"Definitely."

"So you're not fine?"

"No. But more... miserable, than feeling ill, I think."

"Yeah, that's fairly standard, I'm afraid. Anxiety, depression... your brain gets all thrown off. There's a charity that offers stroke counselling - it helped me."

He seemed so confident, she was surprised he had needed counselling. "Oh. Okay. I'll look into that."

He grinned. "So, you've been to Bamburgh before, I presume?"

"Of course! I grew up here, remember?"

"Oh, yeah. I just feel like so many people have never even heard of it."

"I've always loved it. Haven't been in years, though."

"So how long have you lived in Newcastle for?"

She smiled at the fact that he had remembered where she lived, even though it hurt a little to think of the life she had abandoned.

"Since I was eighteen," she said. "Went there for uni, never came back."

"I never fancied living in a city," Sam said. "So busy! Do you not find it too much?"

She laughed and shook her head. "Not really. The buses were a bit confusing to start with, and the traffic noise kept me awake for the first few nights… now I struggle to sleep without it. Have you always lived round here?"

He shook his head; "Grew up on a farm in Yorkshire," he said. "Then Dad got a job in Edinburgh, we lived there for a few years… then they divorced, and I moved to Berwick with Mum when I was eighteen. Trained as a plumber, moved out…moved back in after my stroke," he said, rolling his eyes.

"I know the feeling. Can you still do plumbing?"

"A bit," he said. "I have an assistant, can't always do the physical stuff if it needs both hands." Macy could see it hurt him to admit the weakness, but she was glad he did; she felt like she could at least understand a little of how he felt.

"I wonder if I'll ever feel well enough to live alone again," she said, glancing out of the window as the fields raced by.

"I reckon you will," he said. "Or you'll get so sick of your parents you'll push yourself to!"

Macy laughed, and then felt guilty for doing so.

"No, they've been great…"

"I'm sure they have. Doesn't mean you want to live with them forever!"

"Well, no, I guess not," she said with a smile. "Is your new flat in Berwick too?"

He nodded; "Easier, now I can't drive. And Mum is walking distance away, which makes her feel better."

"That makes sense. And it has a train station, which is always handy!"

"Used to be great for nights out in Edinburgh," he said. "Now… not so much. But yeah, it's useful."

"I can't imagine ever going on a night out again!" Macy said.

"Yeah, it doesn't hold the same appeal, does it. I've been drunk once since my stroke, and the symptoms were so similar I scared myself witless. Not worth it."

"No… doesn't seem like it would be. What else is there to do round here?"

"Did you only get wasted when you lived here as a teen?" he asked, with a laugh. "There's the cinema… walks, although I don't do many of them, and golf is a bit dodgy with my useless hand. But I sit on the beach sometimes… did you not miss the beach, in the city?"

"Yeah," Macy said. "I did actually."

And as the bus stopped right alongside her favourite beach, she was reminded of why she loved it.

◆ ◆ ◆

The sky was a miserable off-white colour, filled with clouds that hopefully were not inclined to drop rain upon the group. Once they had made it onto the sand, Macy took off her shoes and let her toes crunch in it. The sea seemed to go on for miles, but it was the castle behind them that really stole the show. In the shadow of the impressive stone structure, how could this beach seem anything but magical?

She waited for Sam to finish taking his shoes off, and resisted the urge to offer to help when he seemed to be struggling. She trusted he would ask if he needed help; she didn't want to make him feel incapable. She was sure he was very used to coping with the after-effects of his stroke.

"Makes me feel like a kid again, going bare foot on the beach," he said with a grin. "Do you want to do the castle tour?"

Macy shrugged. "I'm not fussed. I'm quite happy on the beach."

He looked at her, and then out to the horizon. "Me too."

There was a frisson of something between them, Macy was sure - but she couldn't quite tell what it was. Friendship? Pity? Shared experience? She glanced at him for longer than was probably appropriate, and then looked up at the castle, pretending that was the intended destination for her eyes all along.

He was cute. There was no denying it. His dark hair made his green eyes seem even brighter, and his smile was distracting. And he seemed to smile a lot.

And she liked that.

"Want to paddle?" he asked.

"It's freezing!"

"So?"

She giggled, and then realised she couldn't remember doing that in the last few weeks. "Go on then."

They made their way down the beach; Macy adjusted her pace as his crutch kept slipping into the sand, but they made it down to where the shingle met the sea. Macy quickly rolled up the hems of her jeans, to avoid them getting soaked, then glanced at Sam in his chinos. Should she offer? Would he be offended? Was it too intimate?

"Do you want me to help roll yours up?" she asked in the end, as the tide pulled out and a big wave was threatening to come in.

"If you don't mind…" he said. His eyes were fixed on the horizon, and she bent and rolled them up as quickly as she could, trying not to let her fingertips graze his calves; trying not to noticed the dark smattering of hair on them, or the hard muscles.

"Thanks," he said, but when she stood up she began to see stars, and grabbed out to steady herself.

The only thing nearby, of course, was him, and her hand landed on his warm arm, bare where he had rolled his sweatshirt sleeves up.

"All right?" he asked.

"I just… I get dizzy, when I stand up too quick."

He nodded. "Me too. It will pass. Do you need to sit?"

"I think I'll be okay," she said, keeping her hand on him. She didn't want to embarrass herself by collapsing here on the wet sand, and yet she didn't want to be reliant on anyone else.

"Sorry…"

"Don't be," he said, just as the water rushed up over

their feet. "God that's cold!"

"Freezing!" she said, feeling her head beginning to clear, and her breathing returning to normal.

She knew she should let go of him, now the danger of passing out seemed to have passed, but she found it hard to force herself to. And when she did lift her hand slightly, he let his crutch fall to the floor, and reached over to put his hand on top of hers, keeping it in place.

And for several minutes they stood like that, wincing and shrieking and laughing every time the surf covered their feet, and wondering if they would get the feeling back in them.

Macy glanced at the castle, then the sea, then at Sam, and she smiled to herself. Life wasn't going to plan, but she would try to rejoice in the fact that, at this moment in time, she felt more at peace with the world than she had done in quite a while. Perhaps even since some time before the stroke.

"Can I buy you some fish and chips?" Sam asked. "And maybe a hot chocolate... to avoid hypothermia."

She smiled; "Go on then."

"Could you get my crutch? But don't go fainting."

She laughed, and bent more slowly to retrieve it. The metal was cold, especially compared to how

Sam's hand had felt on hers, and she wiped it on the hem of her top to make sure he wouldn't slip as soon as he held it.

\* \* \*

Most of the group had gone on the castle tour, but Macy didn't mind the cold. The wind blew and the air was fresh, but she felt more alive than she had in weeks. They walked along the sea front towards a shop selling fish and chips, and Macy tried to ignore all the questions filling her head, and instead enjoy this moment. How many moments in life could be truly enjoyed, without worrying or stressing about what was coming next?

She didn't want to spend the rest of her life scared of what was going to happen.

"What do you do, in Newcastle then?" Sam asked her.

"I work in advertising," she said. "Running digital campaigns."

"Do you enjoy it?"

"I think so… it's not terrible, anyway," she said with a shrug. "The money's pretty good and I can be artistic sometimes."

"You like to be artistic?"

"This feels like an interview!" she said. "I like to paint, in my spare time."

"What sort of things?"

"All sorts. Portraits, at the minute."

"Maybe you can do mine."

"Maybe…if my eyesight sorts itself out."

That stilted the conversation, and she felt guilty about it, as well as sad that her eyesight was still causing her issues.

"Did you always want to be a plumber?" she finally asked, breaking the silence.

"No, I wanted to be a firefighter, but then I realised I'm scared of heights, and not too keen on fire and… well, training as a plumber seemed a better option."

"Do you enjoy it?" she asked, as they reached the little takeaway hatch.

"I did," he said. "When I could do it all myself. Now.. I get frustrated, sometimes. But I'm teaching my assistant at the same time, so I suppose that's a silver lining."

He seemed to be so honest about things, despite the fact that he barely knew her, and she admired that. There was so much she felt she kept buried all the time, not wanting to burden people or make them feel awkward, or even to be vulnerable in front of them.

Would life be easier if she were more honest with everyone? With herself?

◆ ◆ ◆

They sat on the low stone wall by the beach and ate their fish and chips. They had forgone the hot chocolates, but the hot food worked wonders in warming their cold bodies.

"Can I ask you something?" Macy said, knowing that she could not ask anyone else this question.

"I think you just did," he said with a smile, his eyes crinkling as he speared a chip with a little wooden fork. "But yeah, you can ask another!"

She rolled her eyes, and laughed. "It's a bit miserable."

"I can do miserable," he said, putting on a pretend sad face.

"Do you worry… that all this…" She waved her hand in the air, then realised that she probably needed to clarify. "The having a stroke… will stop you being able to live the life you were supposed to?"

"I mean…" He put the fork down and looked at her for a minute. "Yeah, of course. But I'm a few years on now, and it hasn't killed me - so I'm trying to achieve everything I would have done, in spite of it."

"I just worry… I worry I'm not going to get to live a long life, hell, even an acceptable-length life. That I won't get to travel or marry or have kids or do any of the things I thought I was going to do. That I'll just feel scared all of the time…"

She took a breath, realising her words had run away with her. And to this good-looking man she barely knew, too.

"Sorry. Way too heavy," she said, trying to laugh it off.

"I get it," he said. "But you survived. You're here. It's shit that it happened, and recovery is not fun. But you'll reach a point - I reached a point, where I didn't want to live in fear of death all the time. Anything could happen to any one of us, at any time. And that's a terrifying prospect. But it's true for everyone - and a reason to grab the good moments. To make the most of everything."

Macy nodded, trying to take in his words, but not sure she was ready to hear them.

"I'm just so scared…"

"You won't be, forever," he said. "Trust me."

"Okay," she whispered, meeting his eye.

"It's good to talk," he said. "Most people don't get all of this, so use me. Talk to me. I can take it."

❖ ❖ ❖

"Good day?" Mum asked, as they sat on the sofa with their dinner on trays. Exhaustion washed over Macy, but as she thought back, she knew that it *had* been a good day.

"Yeah, it was, thanks."

"Bet it was cold at the beach!" Dad said.

"Freezing," Macy said, picking at the broccoli on her plate.

"Are you going to go on another trip out with them, do you think?"

"I reckon so," Macy said, without needing to think. She had felt more normal today than she had in weeks.

That night in bed she found herself replaying moments from the day: standing in the surf, his hand on her arm, the fish and chips and the heart-to-heart.

It reminded her of having a crush back in secondary school - laying in this bed, thinking about a boy. She had been so focussed on the stroke and how ill and miserable she was that this had snuck up on her, rather unexpectedly. But he was cute, and funny, and he understood her - and she was definitely thinking about him more than she was anyone else in the group.

Her phone lit up as she felt her eyes closing, and she rolled over to grab it from the bedside table. It slipped through her fingers, as things seemed to have a habit of doing lately, and she winced at the sound it made as it hit the wooden floorboards.

She heard footsteps on the stairs, and then her door flew open. Mum looked out of breath, and Macy immediately felt guilty.

"Sorry…" she said. "Dropped my phone. I keep doing that…"

"It's fine," Mum said, breathing heavily. "Just thought you'd fallen."

"Just my phone… think it's under the bed."

"I'll get it," Mum said, kneeling down and fishing under the bed until she grabbed it.

"Sorry for worrying you," Macy said, as she took the phone.

Mum smiled. "It's part of being a mother," she said. "I always worry about you."

"More now, I guess."

"Yes… but that won't last forever." She gave Macy's hand a squeeze. "Love you."

"Love you too Mum. Night."

And then she was gone, and Macy remembered the reason she had been trying to get her phone at all.

Her heart raced as she read the message: *Still owe you that hot chocolate.* There was no name, and she didn't have the number saved, but she was sure it was Sam. She checked back through the group chat and found one from the same number, just to double check it was him.

*You can buy me one when we visit Alnwick.*

She smiled at the fact that he was thinking about her, and knew this cemented her decision to attend the next group trip, to Alnwick Castle. She'd been before, on a school trip - but not since it had been used as a famous film location, and never with someone she had a crush on.

❖ ❖ ❖

In some ways the next fortnight went quickly - and in others it dragged by. There was still no updates from the neurologists, despite several phone calls. They were still testing her blood, and trying to book in other tests... but no real progress. They said they would send some sort of heart monitor - but it wouldn't be quick in coming.

The fear was still in her, but she was finding she could just about live with it.

There had been no messages or phone calls from

her friends, and only one from work - and that was to see if she had a date to return.

It felt like no-one really cared - and that hurt.

It felt like she had spent her adult years on relationships that were as flimsy as paper - and that made her sad..

So she focussed on the upcoming trip to Alnwick Castle, and the thought of a bit of flirtation with Sam. It wasn't a big deal, she told herself. People flirted all the time, looked forward to seeing people, thought they were cute... But it had been a while since she had done so, and this felt different to the awkward dinner dates she had been on in Newcastle, usually because on of her so-called friends had set her up. There was excitement and anticipation in this - and no plan for how to escape if things went sour.

"She seems a bit better," she heard Mum say, on the morning of the trip. It was early, before Dad had left for work, and before Macy was usually up - but she had found today she was awake unusually early, and fancied a cup of tea.

"She does," Dad said, and it was obvious they hadn't heard her coming downstairs.

"I still think she should speak to someone. All this trauma... it's not just physical."

"I know. She'll talk to someone, if she wants to - I'm

sure."

Feeling uncomfortable at overhearing any more, Macy made sure to walk loudly into the kitchen.

"Morning!"

"You're up early, love," Dad said, glancing at the big clock above the kitchen table.

"Couldn't sleep any longer," Macy said with a shrug. "And this didn't used to be early for me…"

"I know," Dad said. "But it's early… you know, since…"

"The stroke. You can say it. Yeah, my body seems to be all messed up." She turned to her mother. "Do you mind dropping me into town to go on that trip this morning?" Her eyesight was still not back to normal, and so her driving herself was unfortunately not yet an option.

"Course not," Mum said with a grin.

It was likely to be cold again, so Macy layered up, with black skinny jeans tucked into long boots, and a roll-neck jumper under her coat. She wanted to look nice, and she knew why that was - but she also didn't want to freeze to death.

When she got to the meeting point, Sam wasn't there, but she had a chat with some of the other group members anyway.

"Any news from your doctors?" Levi asked, leaning against a bollard while they waited.

Macy shook her head; "Not yet. Still waiting for results, apparently. Not sure what is taking so long!"

He tutted and rolled his eyes. "Always seems to. Paperwork, I bet. You're too young for them not to find a reason! Unlike me, they just put mine down to being old and smoking too much." He coughed then, as if to underline the point. "And your vision?"

"Still fuzzy," she said, with a sigh. It had been a long time since she had painted - the longest since she was young, she was fairly sure. But the thought of struggling to do so made her sad, and so she had not tried to pick up a brush.

So many things felt like they lived in the pre-stroke world, and she was scared to open the door to that.

The minibus arrived, and they opened the back doors first to load any wheelchairs. Macy found herself glancing around for Sam. He'd not said he wasn't coming, although there had been no more texts. She found the potential disappointment welling up in her stomach: she had come today because she wanted to see him, even though she wouldn't admit that to anybody.

She was the last to get on the bus, and there were

a few seats free, but she chose one at the front, without anyone beside her.

It was pathetic, but she couldn't quite give up the hope of chatting with him on the journey.

"There's room back here, Macy - you don't have to sit alone!"

"I get a bit travel sick," she said, the first excuse that came to her head. It wasn't a total lie - since the stroke, she did find moving vehicles made her nauseous. But it wasn't the reason for her seat choice.

The group organiser, Lexi, got on then, with big smiles and a rain mac that looked ready for any potential down pour.

"Is that everyone?" she asked, and Macy glanced round, her heart dropping. It was time to leave. He wasn't coming.

Lexi pulled out a list, looked up, then checked it again.

"It looks like-"

"Sorry, sorry," a voice came, and Macy smiled as Sam board the bus, his crutch tapping on the metal runners on the steps, a little out of breath.

"There was a leak," he explained. "In the shop next door. I was trying to help... lost track of time."

"No problem, Sam," Lexi said. "Glad you could make it!"

He took the seat next to Macy, and she was embarrassed that her heartbeat sped up a little. She was a grown woman of thirty, not a teen in the first flush of lust. She hadn't felt so flustered over a boy - man - since she was a teenager.

And then he turned, and grinned at her, and her heart set off racing of its own accord. There was a shadow of stubble across his face, like he had forgotten to shave that morning, and his dark hair looked windswept.

"Hi," she said, feeling a little tongue-tied.

"Hey," he said, laying his crutch on the floor and doing up the lap belt. "Thought I was going to miss it!"

"Me too," she said.

"Were you disappointed?" he asked, a smile on his face and a twinkle in his eye - but he was too close to the truth for Macy's liking.

"Only that I was going to miss out on my hot chocolate again," she said, and he laughed - loudly enough that, for a second, the whole bus seemed to go silent and look, before continuing their conversations.

"Did you fix the leak?" she asked.

"I told someone how to fix it," he said, lifting his right hand and letting it drop back to his lap. "This is not much use, unfortunately, and there's not much I could do one-handed."

"I'm sorry," she said.

He took a deep breath, and then relaxed his left hand, which had been balled up in a fist.

"It's fine. I just hate the reminder of what I can't do anymore… you know?"

Macy nodded. "I do."

"Have you managed any painting yet?"

She shook her head. "My vision is still…off."

"You could try anyway," he said with a shrug. "Or go to the opticians. See if they can do anything to help. They're quicker than the neurologists, that's for sure!"

"Yeah, I should do that," she said, with more conviction than when her dad had suggested the very same thing.

"Try not to let the stroke take things away," he said softly. "Not if you can take them back."

She nodded.

"Sorry. That sounds preachy. I'm in an odd mood this morning."

"It's fine. I can take it." Then she smiled.

"Talk to me about something else," he said.

She thought for a moment; "What about the amount of times my mum has barged into my room, thinking I've had a fall? And that I feel way too young for anyone to say I've, 'had a fall'?"

That made him laugh.

"I want to drive again," she said. "But I don't know if I'll be too scared, even if my vision calms down."

"It's like riding a bike," he said. "Or driving a car." They both laughed; "Get your vision checked, then go from there. It could be anything - after effect of the stroke, something to do with the medication... It's a vicious circle."

"The tour is at twelve," Lexi said, as they approached the Castle. "So you've got about an hour before, to see the grounds, or get something to eat. Then about an hour after, before we head home, okay?"

The chatter on the bus got louder, as people made plans about specifically what they wanted to see: gardens, clocktowers, courtyards and ramparts. Macy was a little embarrassed that she had not thought about what she wanted to see. Only who.

"Shall we get that hot chocolate first?" Sam suggested, and Macy grinned and nodded.

"Sounds like a plan."

❖ ❖ ❖

They sat in the chilly courtyard, their coats zipped up against the wind, and sipped their hot chocolates.

"Do you ever think… what if?" Macy asked, as she watched an archery re-enactment on the other side of the courtyard.

"About the stroke?"

"Yeah… or just the decisions you've made…"

"No," he said quickly, shaking his head. "I don't think there's any point. What's done is done - there's no point thinking about how it could have gone differently. It could have been better - but it could have been worse."

She nodded, letting his words sink in.

"Why, do you?"

"Yeah… but not just about the stroke. About everything. I always thought I would have so many things in place by the time I was thirty, and I haven't."

"Come on," he said. "Let's walk, before we freeze." They left their cups on the table, and began a slow wander towards the castle. "Things will look brighter, Macy - and you have plenty of time to make different decisions, if you don't think they worked out so well the first time."

"Do you not regret anything?"

He laughed; "Of course I do! But I just realised at some point that it's pointless thinking about what might have happened. If I want something to change I need to change it, now."

He spoke a lot of sense - but she wasn't sure exactly what she did want, yet. Other than, perhaps, for this stroke to have never happened - and there was nothing she could do about that.

The tour was more interesting than she expected, and they made their way slowly through each room, looking at ancient suits of armour and grand beds that royalty had once slept in.

When she had come here on a school trip, she remembered - with a smile - just wanting to visit the gift shop. It had always been the most exciting part of the day - but now she found the tour kept her attention better. She did take a moment to glance around at the group, though: Sam walked beside her, listening intently. Levi, Sharon - who was not wearing stilettos this time - and Joan walked together, looking at the guide book occasionally. Lexi pushed Amal, whose wheelchair had been struggling over the uneven flagstones. They were an unusual mix, filling the great hall on this quiet, blustery day. And yet something linked them together, and always would do.

❖ ❖ ❖

"I'm going to make an appointment at the opticians," Macy said, when Mum picked her up later that afternoon. "If you don't mind giving me a lift."

"Great plan, love - of course I don't."

"And ring the neurologist. Again. I want to get things sorted."

Mum grinned, and squeezed her arm before driving them home.

Despite being exhausted, Macy offered to cook that night, and although it was only a simple pasta bake, her parents raved about it.

"Are you feeling a bit better today?" Dad asked.

"Yeah… I think I am," Macy said, finding that she was smiling without even meaning to. "I think… I need to accept what's happened, and figure out how to move past it. Starting with my eyesight. And trying to get some answers."

# CHAPTER SEVEN

Sam had asked the question, as they had talked, and it had stuck in her mind: do you enjoy your job?

She had always thought she did, really. She didn't love it, but she also didn't dread going in. It wasn't her passion, but she also didn't have any strong feelings against it. The people were nice enough, the money was good, and she'd always thought it would be a great job until…

Until what? She wasn't even sure now, what her plan had been. What was the dream?

And then, somehow, years had gone by - and she'd never really revisited any of those questions. Did she like her job? Was she happy in the city? Where did she want to be in a year's time? In five?

She had enough time on her hands to ponder the answers to these questions, and she decided to push herself a bit and go for a walk alone. The footpath round the fields was fairly dry, and she knew at the end of it there was a lovely view of the ocean.

She was going to take headphones, but then decided she wanted to be able to hear herself think. And so, think was what she did, as she spent some very rare time alone. It was strange, really; for years she had spent almost every evening alone, and yet now she was always with someone.

It was easy to distract herself from her thoughts, and easier to feel safe, when people were around.

But there were thoughts she needed to face.

She had decided, at some point when she was talking with Sam, that she was not willing to let this stroke take any more from her than it already had. She had the opticians appointment the following day, and the neurologist had promised her a face to face appointment soon. It had been six weeks since that fateful day, and although she knew recovery wouldn't be quick, she needed to think about getting back to living her life. It couldn't be put on pause permanently.

Her feet trudged on and she realised that it wasn't taking as much effort as it had done in recent weeks. Perhaps it was the distraction of her thoughts; or perhaps she was getting better.

The stile came into view, and she gripped it purposefully, swinging her leg over and coming down the other side. She grinned, even though she was the only one there, and took a few deep breaths. It felt like an achievement - and she was going to clasp those as tightly as she could.

Onwards, along the hedge, towards the ocean.

Did she want to restart her life… the life she had before?

Or did she want a new life?

This felt like a cross-roads, a second chance - and she wanted to grab it. But she didn't know what she wanted to hold onto…

She reached the edge of the field, a little out of breath, and looked down at the glinting ocean, vast and intimidating. It bobbed and swayed, and she watched it until her breath calmed down, and then after that, until she could answer the questions rolling around her head.

*Start small,* she told herself. *Can you see yourself going back to the office?*

The answer to that, she was sure, was no.

Although she had no idea what she might want to do.

A bird dived towards the sea, picked something from it with its beak and then soared away.

*Do you want to live in the city?* Harder this time… but she wasn't sure she wanted to be alone again. She needed some support. Maybe not living with her parents, but perhaps near…

As she made her way back, hoping for a nice cup of tea and a long sit down, she felt a peace settle over her. She didn't really know what she wanted, but she knew what she didn't want -and that was something, right?

❖ ❖ ❖

"Well, Miss Maxwell," the optician said, after making her choose between 'one and two' more times than she could count, "Your eyes look healthy, and your vision doesn't seem to have changed drastically. You'll need to speak with your neurologist, but I would imagine the vision issues are a side effect of the stroke, or the medication."

"They didn't seem to think it would be permanent…"

"Well, your peripheral vision is fine, and glasses won't improve the issues you're having I'm afraid. Do you have an appointment with your neurologist soon?"

Macy nodded: "Next week."

"Definitely ask - lots of things can cause vision issues, see what they can do about it."

"Thank you."

Although it brought no answers, it was another step ticked off the list - and she finally had an appointment to see the neurologist in person, and she would be armed with a long list of questions.

When she got home, Mum and Dad were both out, and she sat in the living room and enjoyed the peace and quiet. She could live nearby, perhaps, she thought - and still get time alone, but see them regularly. And then there were friends from school that she could look up, maybe have a bit more of a network than she had back in the City.

Her phone pinged, and she saw several new messages from the stroke group.

*Next meeting is Wednesday, 10am!*

*See you all there.*

*Any one able to give me a lift?*

She sighed. She found she wanted to go, and not just to see Sam - although there was a certain appeal to that; but she liked hearing other people's stories, and sharing her own, and feeling like people understood.

But Wednesday was her neurology appointment, which Mum and Dad had offered to take her to, and so there was no way she was going to be able to attend the meeting.

*Sorry,* she typed. *Can't make it, but will be at the next outing!*

Seconds later her phoned pinged again, but this

time it wasn't the group chat. It was Sam.

*Shame you can't come Wednesday.*

She took a deep breath and messaged back, grinning as she did so. She didn't know why, but the fact he had messaged her personally, even something so simple, made her happy.

*Finally got a neurology appointment back home.*

But the wording didn't sound quite right, so she sent another message, a clarification.

*In Newcastle.*

It wasn't home any more.

Maybe it never had been.

*Glad you've got an appointment - but I was looking forward to seeing you.*

It was the most openly either of them had acknowledged that they enjoyed one another's company, and it made her giddy.

And it made her want to say the same back.

*Me too,* she typed. *Next time?*

*How about coffee… Friday?*

Her heart sped up, but not in the anxious way she was now used to. She didn't wonder if she was having a heart attack, or check to make sure she could still walk in a straight line.

*Sounds great.*

*There's a cafe on the High Street that's nice - it's called Latte Life. Cheesy name but the coffee's good. 11 good for you?*

*Perfect.*

*It's a date.*

A date.

She put the phone down and resisted the urge to jump up and down because, to be honest, it would only make her feel ill.

A date.

When was the last time she'd had a date?

When was the last time she had been excited about a date?

Perhaps this could actually lead to *something*...

The door opened, and she knew she needed to tamp down her excitement. She couldn't let on that she had a date... not yet. They would be nosy and worried and she just wanted to be excited for now and think about what she would wear and what it would feel like to kiss him...

It seemed living in her teenage home had reverted her to teenage emotions.

But she didn't care.

♦ ♦ ♦

On the morning of her neurology appointment, she found she was unreasonably nervous. They weren't going to do anything, after all - discuss her scans, look at results, answer questions... but she was so eager to get her life back, that the ramifications of these conversations made her nervous.

"Ready love?" Mum asked. "Dad's in the car."

"You don't both have to come..." she said, knowing that at least one of them did, to drive her; she didn't fancy public transport alone yet, and driving still wasn't an option.

"We want to," she said. "And I'll come in with you, if that's okay - you're bound to forget some of your questions!"

Macy nodded. "Thanks Mum."

The drive was longer than she remembered, and she felt queasy sitting in the back, but didn't want to make Mum feel guilty by saying so.

As her parents chatted in the front, Macy focussed on the fields whizzing by, and tried not to throw up. It didn't feel like driving home, as they drove down the A1, and that further compounded her thoughts of not returning to the city to live.

When they arrived, Dad dropped them off at the front door, and circled round to find a parking space. The hospital was busy, but they found their way to the neurology department and checked in, before sitting on metal chairs that were screwed into the ground. Macy had definitely had enough of hospitals. From never really being in them, the visits - and associated phone calls - were becoming far too regular. She just hoped it wouldn't be the case forever.

"Macy, good afternoon," the neurologist - Doctor Histon - said, when they were called in, only ten minutes after the appointment time.

"Hi," Macy said. "This is my Mum."

"Nice to meet you Mrs Maxwell. Please, take a seat. So, Macy, how have you been?"

Macy paused for a minute, knowing it was important to be honest and accurate. The chance to speak with the neurologist probably wouldn't come up again for some time.

"Tired, a lot," she said. "And I keep fumbling with things… and my vision isn't great."

She nodded. "Tell me about your vision."

"It feels blurry, especially when I'm tired. Like my eyes can't focus on things for long. I went to the opticians, but they said there was nothing wrong with my eyes that they could deal with."

The doctor nodded; "The stroke did touch the area that deals with vision, so it could well be that, or the medication. But I think it's unlikely to be permanent. Now, could you walk in a straight line for me? Brilliant, and touch your nose, and my finger…" She rattled through the tests that Macy had done many times over by now, and the doctor made notes after each one.

"So the deficits you have described are definitely not unexpected after the type of stroke you had," the doctor said. "And you generally have very good balance. If your vision hasn't sorted itself in a month, I'd like to have some scans done, but for now it seems you are healing remarkably well. And," she said, clicking to bring up some notes on the screen. "We have a plan to find out the cause of your stroke."

"I haven't had the heart monitor they said about yet…" Macy said, and the doctor frowned.

"I'll chase that up. I think there's a good chance you tore an artery in your neck at some point, which has clotted and then blocked the blood flow to your brain when you had the stroke."

"I thought they looked for that…" Mum said.

"They did," the doctor said. "But it's the most common reason for strokes in young people, and there's nothing in your blood work, Miss Maxwell, that suggests anything else, so I'd like to get a closer look. We'll get a team of neurologists to look at your scans closely and see what we can find. Sometimes it's a tear that is so tiny it's hard to see, but it can still cause major problems."

"And then?" Macy asked, swallowing, feeling like her throat had gone dry. "If that is what it is… then what?"

"Then you can come off the statins, and after it's healed - which usually takes about six months - you can come off the blood thinners too."

"And it won't happen again?" Mum asked.

"It's an unfortunate chain of events that lead to it," she said. "Nothing you could have done, and no reason it would happen again."

"So I'd just.. Go back to normal?"

The doctor nodded; "The fatigue may last longer, but yes, you should do."

"And if it's not that?"

"We'll do more tests. There will be a reason - it's very unusual for a thirty-year-old to have a stroke and no reason be found."

It was unusual to have a stroke at all, Macy thought - but didn't say it.

"We should know if there's a tear in the next

couple of weeks," the doctor said. "And I'll ring you, when we have more information."

"Thank you," Macy said.

Mum linked arms with her and moved her in the direction of the exit. She felt in a bit of a daze.

"It's good news, isn't it love?"

Macy nodded. "Yeah. I think so…"

"I think they'll find that tear, and then you can start planning for the rest of your life."

"Mmhmm."

Mum relayed the information to Dad once they got back to the car, while Macy sat quietly and fiddled with the loose thread on her jumper. It was just too much to process the new information and make conversation. She wanted some time to let everything sink in.

This might all have been something totally random, that would not happen again.

There was a good chance she wouldn't need to spend the rest of her life living in fear.

That she would have a life to live.

She hadn't asked that question that had been haunting her: was a shortened life-span something she would have to accept?

She hoped the doctor's encouraging words meant it wasn't.

"Macy?" Mum said, and their eyes met in the rear-view mirror. "Are you all right?"

"Yeah. Sorry. Just a bit... overwhelmed." It happened a lot lately: too much information or noise or not enough sleep and her brain just seemed to scream *I can't cope!*

"Okay. Just checking."

# CHAPTER EIGHT

She was half an hour early, but the butterflies in her stomach had set her pacing the living room, and she had been making her mum suspicious about this need for a lift, so they had left early.

"So it's your stroke group today?" Mum asked as they drove. She had looked Macy up and down after they left, and she wondered if it was obvious that she had changed her outfit several times. She had ended up with a pair of black skinny jeans, although she had fumbled with the button over and over again, and a black polo neck.

"Yeah."

"I didn't realise they were meeting today?"

"Just a few of us today… separate meeting," she said, tapping her foot and wishing they could hurry up - despite being early.

"That's nice."

In spite of being a good thirty minutes before their planned meeting time, Macy entered the café and glanced around. She didn't think she'd ever been in here – although perhaps she had, under a different name, before some sort of refurbishment. The high street here seem to be always changing – or perhaps nothing ever lasted that long.

He wasn't there, of course, and she contemplated leaving and coming back – but that felt a little awkward. Besides, the weather outside was not pleasant – she might as well wait in here.

She wandered up to the counter and perused the menu on a blackboard above the cashier's head.

"Macy? Macy Maxwell?"

Her head turned towards the sound of her name, and she blinked twice, her brain catching up with the sight before her.

"Amelia?" she said, finally, to a grin from the tall blonde in front of her.

"Yes! I wasn't sure you'd recognise me – it's been so long."

"It has... Years..."

"You just disappeared after you went to Uni. I didn't know you were back."

"I'm not..." Macy began, but then she realised it wasn't entirely true. She was back – had been for a few weeks, and was considering making the move permanent. "I've not been well, so I'm staying with my parents for a while." The truth, even if it was not the entirety of it.

"Oh, I'm sorry," Amelia said. They'd been best friends through primary school, and for a decent chunk of secondary school. She was fairly sure a boy they both liked had been part of the reason they had grown apart, but it was so long ago she barely remembered. And perhaps Amelia was right – when she had gone to university, she left everything behind her, without a backward glance. "I hope you're better now?"

"Getting there..." Macy said. It wasn't something that was easy to get into in a quick five minute conversation.

"Have you got time for a coffee? I'd love to catch up..."

Macy glanced at the clock. Still twenty-five minutes until Sam would be here... She couldn't exactly wait here while telling Amelia no, she was busy... But on the other hand, she did not want seem occupied when he arrived.

"I'm meeting someone at eleven," she said.

"I've gotta leave by eleven – but I'd love to catch up now, if you've got time?"

She had forgotten how much she liked Amelia. She had always been quite quiet, and unassuming – but she was always respectful, and sweet, and had never pushed past any boundary that Macy had put up.

They bought drinks and moved to a table in the corner, where they awkwardly smiled at each other for a minute.

"So how have you been?" Macy asked, happy to not talk about herself for a little while.

"Good, thanks. I live over in Coldstream, but Mum still lives here."

"That's nice," Macy said, trying to think of what to ask next.

"She's not been well… For a while. So I stay nearby, check on her regularly."

"I'm sorry," Macy said, sincerely. She remembered Amelia's mum as being kind, and that she had always brought a plate of biscuits up to them when they were sat chatting up in Amelia's bedroom.

"It is what it is," Amelia said. "But tell me – what's life like in the city?"

Macy shrugged; "Not all it's cracked up to be," she said, before realising that her words gave away far more of her feelings than she had intended. "To be honest, I think I'll probably move back here."

"I'm sorry it's not working out, but it'll be great for you to be living back up here – there's a group of us who meet here fairly regularly. I'm not sure you would know anyone else, but we're all about the same age – about to turn the dreaded thirty - but then, of course, you already have, haven't you?"

Macy nodded with a sad smile; it wasn't something she particularly liked to think about.

"Anyway, there was a girl I met at work, then she had a friend, and before you know it, there's a group of us meeting once a week to chat about the world and complain about how hard it is to be thirty – or nearly thirty – and not be able to afford a house, find a man, or still to be living with our parents, blah blah blah. You get the picture. But it's a nice group of people, and it'd be an easy way to make friends if you're moving back here."

"Thanks," Macy said with a smile. "That sounds… Nice. I realised recently that the friends I thought I had weren't as good as I thought they were. If that makes sense."

Amelia nodded, "You mean when you are ill?" She was clearly keen to know more about the situation, but didn't want to ask – but Macy suddenly felt it was easier to get all the cards on the table. This would be a part of her forever now; although hopefully not her defining feature.

She nodded; "I had a stroke. I know – imagine how surprised I was. So I've been recuperating my parents, and realised that they're the only ones who are always going to be there for me."

"That's terrible, Macy, I'm sorry – how are you

doing now?"

"Getting there," Macy said with a shrug. "Can't drive yet, and don't have a reason yet, but I'm hoping I'll get there eventually. They seem to think I'll recover completely, in time."

"Well, that's something. But still, what a nightmare."

Macy certainly wasn't going to argue with that.

She glanced at the clock and realised that it was very close to eleven – and somehow she had been distracted from her half an hour of worrying. Amelia glanced up too.

"Look, I'm sorry, but I've got to run – Mum is expecting me. But here –" She rummaged in her handbag for a pen and scribbled onto a napkin. "Here's my number. Can we do this again? Even if it's just us two – although I think you'd quite like the group."

"Sounds great. I'll text you, yeah? It was really great to see you." To her surprise, she found she meant it. Maybe it was the nostalgia, or just the feeling of connecting with somebody else, but she felt like she wanted more time to spend with Amelia.

"Brilliant. And take care of yourself, Macy, okay?"

Macy nodded, and once Amelia had left she only had three minutes in which to work herself up into a frenzy of nerves before the door opened, the bell above it tinkled, and Sam walked in.

❖ ❖ ❖

"Am I late?" he asked, glancing at her empty coffee cup.

She laughed, and shook her head. "I was early, and ran into someone I went to school with!"

"Another coffee?"

"Tea, if that's okay?"

He nodded and went up to the counter, which gave her a chance to look at him without blushing furiously. She hoped they offered to carry it over, for she didn't think it'd be possible to carry two drinks with his crutch.

His dark hair sat against the back of his neck, a couple of small curls tucking into the back of his polo shirt. It was navy, and he wore a leather jacket over it, with black jeans and black boots.

A rush of hormones washed over her and she was very much reminded of her nerves about this date.

A waitress followed him with the tray - two drinks, and two brownies. Macy could see she was checking him out, but she disappeared once she'd put the tray on the table.

"Thanks," she said.

"I can eat both brownies, if you don't want one," he said.

"I love brownies."

"So... how was your appointment?"

Macy smiled; "Good, I think. They're looking to see if I have an artery tear, and if I do... things should return to normal, at some point."

He smiled; "That's great. And how's life with your parents?"

"Not too bad! But part of me wonders if I'm ready to move out. I don't want to get to the point where they're fed up of me... or vice versa."

He laughed; "Mum and I reached that point - don't worry, we've recovered from it now that I live alone. So will you go back to the city?"

"I..." she paused. Nothing had been decided, and she wasn't sure of her plans yet; she didn't want to give him false hope. But was that reading too much into this situation? They had gone out for coffee - that didn't mean he was going to be cut up if she moved home. "I'm not sure. I don't think... I don't think I want to go back to my job." That was safer - and something she could honestly say. "I've realised..."

She looked up, and he was watching her, listening to every word, just waiting for her to answer.

"I don't love it. And this stroke... it's made me realise life is short. I know, I know, such a cliché. But I could have died that night, and who knows what else might happen - so I don't want a job where I'm just counting down the hours until home time, or the weekend."

"That makes sense," he said, sipping his coffee. "Any idea what you want to do?"

She shook her head. "I was never one of those girls who had a whole life plan, or knew what she wanted to be when she grew up. I just fell into advertising... The only thing I've ever really enjoyed is my art."

"Could you make a living from that?"

Macy blushed, and shook her head. "I'm not good enough. And now, with my vision... but maybe something related to art."

"I'll have a think."

"I just feel that this stroke... it's made me reconsider everything. Now I'm a bit less angry about it all happening, I can see there's things I would have been pretty gutted about, if that had been the end."

"I felt the same," he said. "Physically, with my arm and leg being so weak... there's a lot of things I wish I'd done."

"Like?"

"Had a motorbike... I know, cliché, mid-life crisis, and I never did because my mum always told me they were death traps but, hey, I nearly died from a stroke in my early thirties, so the odds aren't always in your favour."

"I've never been on a motorbike," she said. "Always been too scared!"

"And I remember wishing... sorry, this is starting to sound like a therapy session!"

"I don't mind," Macy said. In truth, she liked it; talking with Sam was the most honest she had been in weeks, and she felt like he was truly being honest with her in return, rather than trying to shield her from things.

"That I'd met someone. Settled down. Had kids... Before I became useless."

"You're not useless, Sam," Macy said, hating to hear the misery in his voice. She reached out and put her hand on his, to try to take some of the pain away, and he looked up. Their eyes met, and something jolted through her that was a far cry from sadness or pain. He turned his hand beneath hers, so they were palm to palm, and then closed his fingers around hers.

It was thrilling, and yet felt totally right.

And somehow she kept on talking, even as they held hands 0n the table top like teenagers.

"You've made me feel so much better. And you can still do so much. One day, you'll ride on that motorcycle - and meet someone, and get married, and have kids, and…"

"Thanks, Macy. I was meant to be cheering you up…"

"I'm okay," she said, and for once she meant it.

"I'm glad."

"I think… I think I can see the light at the end of all this. I think it's going to change my life totally - but maybe in a good way. I think… I wasn't the person I wanted to be. I've got a second chance."

"That's a very positive way of looking at it."

"It's all your pep talks that have got me seeing things more positively." She reached with her other hand for the brownie, and took a bite, not letting go of his hand.

He grinned, and looked at the brownie, then slowly opened his mouth.

She laughed, nearly choking on the crumbs, before reaching up to offer him a bite of the same brownie. She could feel the warmth of his lips, just millimetres away from her fingers, and felt a strong urge to brush against them, before she remembered they were in a public place.

She lowered the brownie.

"Delicious."

She nodded, her throat dry, words escaping her for a moment.

"Do you fancy a walk?" he asked. "The rain stopped before I came in, and I don't think it's meant to start again."

"Okay," she said, pleased that there was no need to tell him that she got exhausted if she walked too far: he got it. He probably felt the same.

Sam wrapped the brownie in the napkin it was laying on, and put it in his pocket. He didn't let go of Macy's hand as he stood, his other hand propped on his crutch, and they walked out together, with a call of thanks over their shoulders as they left.

Hand-in-hand, they crossed the road, and entered the park that Macy remembered sitting and eating chips in with her mates after school. It was steep, and they took the path slowly, never letting go.

She couldn't quite believe they were holding hands. Nothing had been said, and yet his hand was around hers, and it felt right. It made her feel giddy, and not in the stroke way she was used to. She wondered if she should question it, but they were both free and single adults, and it felt nice.

So she didn't.

"Where's the best place you've ever travelled to?" she asked suddenly, finding the silence as they wended their way down to the path that ran along the River Tweed a little uncomfortable.

"I visited Iona, off Scotland, once, and loved it," he said. "Is that boring? Too close to home?"

She laughed; "No. I've never been, but I've heard it's beautiful."

"How about you?"

"New York," she said, without thinking. "I went when I was nineteen, with some uni friends, and it was... the buildings are so huge, you feel insignificant, but I loved it."

"My turn," he said with a grin. "Favourite food?"

"Pizza," she said, as they walked through the gate and the river twinkled and swayed before them. "You?"

"Hot dogs."

"Cinema trip or bowling?"

"Cinema."

"Me too."

They reached a bench, and Macy paused. "Can we

sit?" Even walking that distance had drained her, and she already felt a little light-headed from the rush of holding his hand, of walking next to him, of this conversation…

He nodded, and they sat. "It's beautiful here," she said.

"Always been one of my favourite walks," he said. "From when we first moved here. And when a train goes across…"

"I always forget how impressive it looks."

She glanced at their entwined hands on the pale wood of the park bench.

"Sam… what are we doing?"

"Walking. Well, we were - now we're sitting."

She smiled, but she was sure he knew what she was asking. She wasn't sure any part of her was strong enough for a miscommunication right now, and it felt like he was an important part of her recovery.

"I mean…" she said, squeezing his hand, and then he looked down, and looked back at her.

"I don't know," he said. "Do you want it to stop?"

"No," she said, honestly. "I feel like a teenager again…"

A smile lit up his face. "Me too. I like you, Macy - and I feel like I can talk to you… like no-one else."

"Me too…"

"But I know you're fragile right now, and your stroke is so recent, and I don't want you to feel I'm taking advantage of you…"

"I don't."

"But I really like your company. And I really like holding your hand."

"Me too," she whispered, hardly daring to say it. A couple walked past with a yappy dog, and they drew their feet in a little.

"I feel dizzy," she said.

"Are you all right? Do you need-" She cut him off, realising he had thought she meant in a stroke way.

"In a good way," she said.

"Oh."

A butterfly landed on a shrub growing in the concrete of the river bank, and then flew off, and they watched it go, letting the weak winter sun seep into their bones.

"So…" Macy said.

"So…"

She laughed, but it was an awkward laugh. "I haven't felt this nervous around a boy since I was a teenager."

"I haven't been this tongue-tied round a girl since *I* was a teenager."

"You don't seem tongue-tied," she said, glancing at him again. The sun sparkled off his green eyes, his beautiful smile, that dark hair that almost seemed to reflect it right back.

"Macy…" he said, and she felt herself losing any resolve to remain on friend-only terms with him. There was something in his voice…

"Yeah?" Her mouth was dry, and their eyes were locked, and the whole town could have been parading past in tartan and she didn't think she would have noticed.

"Can I kiss you?"

She nodded, butterflies of her own filling her stomach, and then her eyes fluttered closed as he let go of her hand, and pressed his palm to her cheek instead. Then he leant in, and she met him, and he smelt like peppermint, and coffee, and chocolate brownie. And then his lips met hers and she was fairly sure a sigh escaped her lips, because she didn't think anything had ever felt so incredible as the moment his soft lips moved with hers, his strong hand holding her face close, her hands moving of their own accord and pressing into his back, between his shoulder blades, pulling him tighter.

She was in danger of losing her grip on the reality of their public location, but when their lips pulled apart, their foreheads fell together, and they breathed in sync for a few minutes.

"That was-"

"Wow."

"Yeah."

Had a first kiss ever set her alight like that? She didn't think so. Was it this connection they had? Or was it something about him? His good looks, or fate, or something… there had to be some reason that the kiss had burnt away every negative thought in her mind and made her think only of him. Of kissing him again. Of being alone with him. Of…

As quickly as that kiss had begun, dark clouds gathered above them, and in true Northumberland style, a sunshine-filled moment turned quickly to one with a threat of a downpour.

"We should get going," he said. "It'll take me a while to get up that hill. You might have to save yourself!"

"I won't leave you," she said, and she took his hand, and grinned.

◆ ◆ ◆

By the time they made it back to the top of the gardens, the rain clouds had opened and they were both soaked to the bone. Several times, Sam suggested she go ahead, but she stuck to her word, and although their hands were cold and wet, they were still clasped together by the time they reached the shelter of a bus stop on the main road.

"Sorry…" Sam said.

Macy grinned, and wiped rain from her cheeks. Not bringing a coat had - as was generally the case in Northumberland - been a mistake. "You don't control the weather!"

They laughed, and took a seat in the bus stop, catching their breath.

Macy felt like she was floating. All the aches and pains, worries, exhaustion - it paled into comparison next to the joy she was feeling. The smile on her face felt like it might be permanent.

"How are you getting home?" he asked.

"My mum's picking me up," she said. "Now I really sound like a teenager!"

He laughed. "Is she coming at a specific time or…?"

Macy shook her head. "Just whenever I ring."

"Do you want to come back to my place to dry off? It's not far-" He seemed to realise what his words implied, and started to back track. "I actually mean to dry off. You're soaked, I don't want you getting ill - I could lend you something to wear, or…"

Macy laughed. "That sounds like a good plan. And a hot drink, if you're offering?" She definitely wasn't ready for more than kissing - but drying off and a hot drink sounded good, especially before she had to face Mum's inevitable questioning.

He nodded; "Definitely."

The walked as quickly as they could through the rain, their hands not separating until they reached a door and Sam had to rifle through his pockets for his keys.

They walked through the bright red front door, and down a hallway with several photos up on either side.

"My mum decorated," he said, with a laugh.

There was an open plan living room and kitchen, and then other doors that she presumed led to the bedroom and bathroom.

He disappeared, and returned with two fluffy blue towels, one of which he passed her. "I'll find you some clothes…"

"If you've got a t-shirt, or a jumper..." she said. "The jeans will be okay." In truth they were rather uncomfortable, but she didn't want to go home in trousers that weren't hers, for there would be far too many questions. Besides, at this point they felt rather like a second skin, and she was fairly sure taking them off - especially with her fumbling hands - was going to be a bit of a challenge. And not one she wanted him to help with.

As she squeezed the water in her hair out into the towel, he quickly dried his, leaving it ruffled, before flicking the kettle switch on and leaving the room again. She heard his crutch on the wooden floor of the hallway, then a door opening. She glanced round the room; the sofa was covered with a fluffy throw, and a large TV took up most of one wall. There were a couple of books on the coffee table, and an unfinished glass of water, but other than that it was very tidy.

"Are these okay?" he asked, holding up a dark grey hoodie and a navy t-shirt. They would be a little long and baggy on her, but they would be a lot warmer and dryer than what she was currently wearing.

"Great, thanks," she said.

"You can change in my room..." he said, and she went in the direction he pointed, suddenly feeling a little shy.

She stripped off, even removing her bra as it was soaked too, and quickly donned the t-shirt and hoodie. They were soft and smelt of detergent, and she immediately felt better. As she folded up her wet clothes, with the bra hidden in the middle, she glanced around his room. Again, it was neat, with navy bedding and matching curtains. The bed was made, and there was another book on the bedside table, along with a medicine box.

When she re-entered the living room, he was stood in the little kitchen, two matching mugs on the side.

"Tea or coffee?"

"Tea, please," she said. She loved both - there was no rhyme or reason to which she chose, but this afternoon definitely felt like a tea moment.

"Sorry about the rain," he said.

"Again - controlling the weather is not one of your many talents!"

"Many talents, hey?"

She blushed, and he didn't push it further. Was he thinking of that kiss as much as she was?

"If you want to ring your mum, feel free," he said, carrying her tea over, before returning for his drink. She sat on one of the dining chairs, aware that her wet jeans would probably leave marks on the sofa.

"I'll drink this first," she said with a smile.

"Don't want her to find you here?"

"I-" It was true, but not perhaps for the reasons he would think. "I didn't mention who I was meeting."

"Don't think she'd approve?"

"Why would she not approve?"

"Fellow stroke victim, weak arm and leg, only recently moved out of his parents house - not sure I'm such a catch."

"You are speaking to a recent stroke victim still living with her parents, remember," she said. "And you are a catch - that's not it. She'll just... ask a million questions, if I let anything on."

He grinned, and took a seat next to her. "I get that."

"I'm not... hiding... whatever this is."

"Would it be acceptable if I took you on a proper evening date next week?" he asked. "Or is that too difficult to explain to your parents?"

She blushed, and glanced down at her tea, before looking back at him. "That would be nice. I'll tell them the truth... but just so you realise, I will have to be dropped off at this date by my mother, so make sure you include that in the tally of who's a catch."

"Well, I can walk there, because I made the sensible decision to live in town," he said. "I wish I could pick you up…"

"No point dwelling on what could have been," she said, echoing his own words of wisdom from the beach. "And this way, we can both have a drink, if we want."

"Need to be drunk to be around me?" he asked.

"I think you know that's definitely not true."

"Maybe you're a day drinker."

She sipped her tea; "Strictly tea and coffee in the day," she said. "I promise."

# CHAPTER NINE

There had been a lot of questions, on the way home, but Macy thought she had managed to dodge them fairly successfully. Why was she wet? They had taken a walk. Who was there? She had distracted from this by mentioning that she had run into Amelia, who her mum remembered from Macy's school days.

Whether she alleviated all her Mum's suspicions, she wasn't sure, but once they were home, and she changed into her own dry pyjamas, there were no more questions. She folded Sam's t-shirt and hoodie neatly and smiled as she looked at them. She probably should wash them, but that would invite questions, so she left them folded beneath her own clothes on a chair, to be dealt with later.

She slept better that night than she had done a long time, feeling warm and comforted despite the amount of time she had spent in wet clothes.

They had plans to go on a proper date – and she was excited about that. He knew that she currently lived with her parents, that she'd had a stroke, that she wasn't sure what she wanted to do with her life... And yet he was still interested. Yes, he had his own baggage, but he was cute, and kind, and funny, and wise – and she found she craved spending time with him. When she was around him, it was almost like he was the sun, and she had spent far too long in the dark. She wondered what it would be like to spend the rest of her life feeling like she was in a sunbeam, and then shook herself, for thinking far too far ahead.

If this stroke had taught her anything, it was that you had to take things a day at a time – no matter how excited you were about them.

She went through her morning routine the next day in a bit of a daze. That kiss they had shared on the bench, and even the far more chaste one he had given her to say goodbye, replayed in her head on repeat while she put some washing on, ate her breakfast, and double-checked her calendar to make sure there were no hospital appointments she was forgetting about.

While she ate, she found herself doodling on a blank section of an advert in a magazine her mother had left out. It was only a simple drawing – a boat on a river, with thunderclouds above it – but it was the closest thing to art she had done a long time, and it made her smile. Then it made her think... Were things getting a little clearer? Was the fuzziness in her sight finally starting to recede?

She tried not to hope, but she thought that perhaps

it was.

For the first time in a while, she decided to open her laptop, and check her emails. Work had stopped checking on her, especially since her sick note still had another three weeks to go, but she knew she would need to be making decisions soon.

Except... She was fairly sure she'd already made her decision. About her job, anyway. Life was too short for a job she didn't enjoy, and wherever she was going to live, she wanted to enjoy what she did.

Her email inbox was overwhelmingly busy, and she scrolled through quickly trying to read and delete anything unimportant, to whittle down what she had to go through. There were a couple from work, but they were old, and she was pretty sure she had spoken to her boss since they been sent anyway. If she handed in her resignation, she suppose she could just email them... She wasn't even sure they'd be that surprised. They certainly weren't struggling without her, it seemed – she was replaceable, which she had always known, but which was much more obvious now.

One email, from only two days previously, was not one she expected. The subject read 'Exciting new opportunity' and was from an email address she did not recognise. She opened it, and read it through three times before truly understanding what it was about.

*Dear Miss Maxwell,*

*My name is Joseph Prince, and I'm the CEO of a new, but fast growing, advertising company in Newcastle – Prince Creatives. I am writing to you because your name has been mentioned several times by people in the industry, who believe you might be undervalued in your current position.*

*I hope this does not seem forward, but after many good reports, I would like to ask you to come and discuss joining us as the chief of design in our Newcastle branch. We can offer a competitive salary if you choose to join our team.*

*Many thanks for your time,*

*Joseph Prince*

She had never heard such glowing things about herself. It was hard to believe that people knew who she was, that people had seen her work, that people felt she could do more. And she supposed she had always thought that she could do more – but she hadn't pushed herself to. The job was comfortable, and well-paying, and she could do it without really thinking.

But perhaps she could do more.

This Joseph guy seemed to think so. He seemed to trust the word of others enough that he was suggesting he might want her for a management position, where she could use her artistic creativity, and not be stifled by anyone else. And a competitive salary… That sounded very promising.

And she did want to quit her job.

But it was in Newcastle… And she had all but made up her mind to move back to Northumberland. To live near her parents… To live near Sam…

Was she being ridiculous? The idea of turning down the possibility of a dream job – or at least, a very impressive job, that she thought she might enjoy – because of a guy she'd been on one date with?

But it wasn't just that. She knew it wasn't. She didn't want to be isolated anymore; she wanted to have friends, her parents close, a boyfriend, one day a husband – life was too difficult to go through it all alone. She had learnt that the hard way.

And yet… This had dropped into her inbox, was being offered to her on a plate. She hadn't even had to search for it – was it a sign? A sign to quit her job? A sign to move back to Newcastle, to start over? It left her thoughts in even more disarray than usual.

❖ ❖ ❖

It was a good job Dad was at work and Mum had

gone to the supermarket, for Macy found herself staring at the laptop screen for well over an hour, unable to decide what she wanted. She wasn't ready to talk about it with anyone... she couldn't bear to disappoint them, or make them sad.

She just needed to know what to think.

About ten minutes before Mum returned, she made one decision, and decided to action it immediately, before she had a chance to ruminate over it, with days of stress and uncertainty.

She pulled the laptop closer, grinned when she realised she could see the screen far better than she expected, and began to type.

*Dear Mike,*

*I'm sorry to do this in an email. Due to my ill health, I do not feel I can return to my position, even once my sick note has expired. Thank you for all your support over the years; I would like this to be considered my official letter of resignation. I can post one to you if you require it.*

*Many thanks,*

*Macy Maxwell*

She hit send and closed the lid before she could think about it anymore.

The email was a bit of a stretch - Mike had never offered a great deal of support, and had practically ignored her since the stroke - but it was polite and professional, she hoped.

She needed money, and somewhere to live - but she knew she didn't want to be in that job, and so at least it was one decision made.

After all, if she wanted it, there was a job waiting for her in Newcastle.

Or a home here.

Mum opened the front door with a cheery hello, and she pushed it all from her mind.

One big decision was enough for a morning.

◆ ◆ ◆

*Is Tuesday night good for you for our date? I know the weekend is traditional but... it feels very far away.*

She grinned at the message that pinged onto her phone on Sunday morning. She was officially unemployed, although no-one aside from her ex-boss knew that yet. There was no reason she couldn't go on a date on a Tuesday night - as long as she could get a lift from her mother.

*Tuesday is great.*

Monday was a stroke group meeting, so she assumed she would see Sam then anyway, although it wasn't quite the same as being alone. Still, she was excited about it - even though she was worked up about the job offer that she had no idea what to do with.

Late on Sunday night, after Mum had cooked a huge roast and they had watched a war film that Dad had been going on about, Macy decided to email them, to at least let them know she had read it. Then she would give it a few days - a week, perhaps - before deciding anything final.

*Dear Mr Prince,* she typed, once everyone else was in bed.

*Thank you for your flattering email. I am very intrigued by your suggestion, and will have to take some time to consider it. I hope it is acceptable if I let you know by the end of the week.*

*Best wishes,*

*Macy Maxwell*

She pressed send, and then closed the lid, pushing the decision out of her mind for the time being.

◆ ◆ ◆

"Could you drop me off to the pub again for the stroke group?" she asked her Mum on Monday morning. "In an hour or so? And then tomorrow evening, I was going to go out for dinner in town, if you don't mind giving me a lift? I can try to get a taxi back, but you know what they're like!"

"It's fine," Mum said, putting her cross stitch down while they spoke. "And Dad can come and get you if I'm tired. Who are you having dinner with?"

"A friend from stroke group," she said, sure she was blushing. "Also, Amelia - Rockwell, who I ran into the other day - said about meeting up with her and a few friends at a café in town at some point."

"That would be nice," Mum said with a smile. "It's nice to see you socialising, and feeling a bit better." Macy hoped the distraction tactics had worked - and it wasn't even a lie. She was planning on meeting up with Amelia; she just hadn't got the guts to text yet. She wasn't sure why it made her anxious, but it did.

"Yeah. I think it will be good. I feel... like things are improving."

"We're so pleased, love," Dad said, from his arm chair. He was having a rare morning off, and it was nice to see him relaxing.

"Even if it means you're just taxiing me around?" she asked with a smile.

"Even then," Dad said.

"I think my vision is improving," she said. "I'm hoping... I think I'll be able to drive soon."

"That's wonderful!" Mum said. Macy felt like she was trying to avoid getting too excited about these improvements. Did she not trust them? Or had Macy been miserable so long, she didn't know how to act?

"I've made a decision," she said suddenly, feeling like it was time to share. "I don't want to go back to my old job."

"Oh?"

"I didn't enjoy it, and, well… life's too short."

"It definitely is," Mum said.

"So I'm going to find something else." She didn't tell them she had already quit; they would only worry about her. And then she'd have to explain the other job possibility, and all the other complicated conversations that would bring up…

"Do you have any idea what you want to do?" Dad asked.

Macy shrugged. "Something artistic, I think. I just… don't want to spend my life wishing for the weekends."

"Well, we'll support you, whatever you decide."

❖ ❖ ❖

"Macy!" Lexi, the group organiser, called as she entered the pub where the group was gathered. "How are you? We missed you last week."

Macy smiled at the warmth she exuded. "Sorry, I had a hospital appointment. I'm doing better, thanks," she said. She felt Sam's eyes on her in the corner of the room before she even spotted him, and when their eyes met, they both grinned.

"Come and sit," Levi said, gesturing to the empty chair next to him, and she hoped Sam wouldn't mind. He was sat with a couple of older ladies that she didn't remember the names of, anyway - and she was sure they would find time to speak.

"How are you?" she asked Levi.

"Oh you know. Same old, same old. But no worse. And you?"

"Things seem to be improving, actually," she said, feeling positivity sweeping through her. The sun had been shining that morning for once and it had only added to her good mood.

"That's good to hear! Have they figured out what caused it yet?"

"Not quite... but they think they're on to something."

"Glad to hear it. Not right, young people having strokes..."

She saw Sam get up and head to the bar, and decided she needed a drink too.

"Can I get you a drink, Levi?" she asked. "I'm desperate for one."

"Coffee, if you don't mind. Black."

"No problem."

She forced herself to walk slowly, although knowing he was stood round the corner, alone, at the bar, made her speed up.

He was leaning against the polished mahogany, his crutch loose on one arm, his other elbow on the bar. His black hair was tousled, and he wore a pale yellow jumper that reminded her of spring.

She stood next to him, and smiled when he turned his head.

"Hey," he said.

"Hey."

"Glad you didn't get ill after being caught in the rain."

"Takes more than that to finish me off - I've survived a stroke, don't you know?"

They both laughed. "Oh, really? I had no idea."

The guy behind the bar came over. "Two coffees, please," she said, "One with milk."

He nodded and headed over to the coffee machine.

"Two coffees?" he said. "Late night?"

She laughed; "One's for Levi."

"Is he stealing your attention?"

She grinned and blushed, but didn't have time to answer before Lexi joined them at the bar. Always chirpy, she practically bounced over, before ordering a hot chocolate.

"The weather's nice today," she said, conversationally.

"Yeah, so much better."

"Hopefully no more downpours like the other day!" Sam said, and Macy knew she was blushing, even though Lexi didn't have any idea of the connotations.

"No, that was unexpected, wasn't it - I was glad I was at home!"

Macy almost jumped as she felt Sam's fingers grazing against her hand as it hung by her side. She tried not to make any sign that she had felt him, but then he was there again, with a little more pressure that time, and she felt like her hand was aflame. Her heart had sped up, and yet she still had to maintain a conversation with Lexi.

"Yeah, I got caught in it - wished I had a coat!"

Lexi smiled, and Macy wondered how long the

coffees could take. She enjoyed the frisson between her and Sam, but she didn't really want to be the topic of gossip in the group if they got wind that something was going on between them, and she wasn't sure how well she could hide the attraction between them if they were this close.

"How are you doing, Sam?" Lexi asked. "I feel like I haven't got to speak to you properly in a while."

"Pretty good," he said. "Living on my own again is a blessing."

Macy read a subtext into that, too, but did not say anything.

"I bet!"

The coffees were put down before her, and Macy paid, before taking her leave, her voice a little more high-pitched than it was normally.

She left them to speak and didn't look back, although her mind was full of Sam, and she struggled to focus on any other conversations for the rest of the hour.

Once everyone had discussed the next outing and said their goodbyes, Macy found herself sitting in the sunshine on a bench at the front of the pub, putting off texting Mum for a lift for a few more minutes.

Sam had been deep in conversation with Sharon

about a plumbing issue she was having, so Macy had not had chance to say goodbye - and although she would be seeing him the following day for their date, she would have been lying if she hadn't acknowledged that she was partly waiting on the bench in the hope of seeing him before she left.

It wasn't long before her patience was rewarded, and he sat beside her in the weak spring sunshine. "I didn't mean to keep you waiting…" he said.

"I wasn't waiting for you!" she answered, hoping he didn't think she was being clingy or desperate. After all, they'd been on one coffee date and shared a kiss, or two - she didn't want to over-think it.

"Sorry… if I made you uncomfortable in there," he said.

Confusion took over her face, and he explained a little more.

"At the bar… you seemed a bit spooked. Sorry, I shouldn't have…"

"No, no, it's fine," she said quickly, feeling bad that she had made him worry. "You just… make it hard to think about anything else."

They both grinned, and both blushed.

"But I shouldn't have… I didn't want to embarrass you."

"I wasn't embarrassed," she said, realising that he

was misreading her reaction. "I just... I don't know what this is, and I didn't want..." She struggled to make herself clear without sounding like a teenage girl in the midst of a crush.

He lay his hand palm upwards on his own knee, and she didn't hesitate before placing hers on top.

"Sorry, I.... thought I messed up."

"I thought I messed up."

For a few minutes they sat silently in the sun, hands entwined, not caring who saw them.

"I think my eyesight's getting better," Macy finally said.

"That's brilliant," he said, and squeezed her hand.

"Any idea where I can get art supplies round here? The shop I used to buy from has closed down."

He nodded; "Yeah, there's a place I walk past a lot - I can show you now, if you want."

"You've got time?"

He nodded; "I need to get to a job in about an hour, but it's on my way home."

"Thanks."

She didn't know where the whim had come from but she didn't want to ignore it. If she could start her art again, and get back to driving... maybe she could be on the road to properly recovering from this.

It was a small shop, with a large window displaying beautiful prints and the resources that had been used to create them. A little bell dinged as Macy opened the door, and Sam followed her in.

"Can you get home okay from here?" he asked.

She nodded; "Yeah, I'm fine - thank you, though."

"See you tomorrow?"

She nodded; "I'm looking forward to it." Then he pressed a brief kiss to her lips and was gone, leaving her a little dazed, and very slow to answer the owner's question:

"Can I help you?"

❖ ❖ ❖

A panicked phone call from her Mum made Macy feel bad that she had spent so much time in the shop. She had forgotten how much she loved to browse paints and papers and canvases, and how exciting it was to have all that possibility ahead. Although she had a rather uncertain future, financially, she had barely spent anything for the last few weeks, and so could afford to splurge on some art materials.

She was perusing the notice board when her phone

began to ring, and she was so engrossed she didn't manage to fish it out of her pocket in time.

*Art lessons by local teacher. All abilities. Contact 07417562386*

*Help wanted in busy art shop. Apply within.*

*Missing cat - black and white, with white patch over eye. Call 07563282956 if sighted.*

*Designer required for local business. Email josie.white@net.com for more information.*

When she tried to reach her loud phone, she fumbled and dropped it, as usual, and so it had rung off again by the time she realised it was Mum ringing - and how late it was.

Carefully carrying her purchases, she said thank you and left to ring her mum back.

"Macy? Are you all right?"

"Yeah, I'm fine… sorry," she said quickly.

"You've been hours. I was worried…"

"I'm sorry, I went to an art shop and got distracted…" She felt terrible for making her mum worry, whilst also wanting to scream that she was thirty and capable of being alone.

But she understood her Mum's worry, and felt guilty for amplifying it.

❖ ❖ ❖

Mum was quiet when she picked her up, and Macy's guilt did not disappear.

"I just lost track of time… it's been so long since I've looked at art supplies."

Mum smiled weakly. "It's okay."

"But I can see you're stressed, and I'm sorry, I didn't mean to…"

"I know you didn't," Mum said. "I'll be okay. It's just…no, it's fine."

"Go on, say what you wanted to say."

"It sounds ridiculous."

"I don't care."

Mum sighed, and then continued. "Fine. I know how terrible this has all been for you, and I am not comparing in any way - but I've been terrified. Every moment of every day. Having a child… it's always terrifying. They're part of you, and then they're not, and it's like having your heart walking around by itself, with its own free will and so many chances to get hurt. I was terrified when I sent you to school, and when you went to uni, and… so many times. But this… this is a fear like

I have never known, and this afternoon, not being able to contact you… I just pictured the worst."

"I'm sorry Mum," Macy said again.

"I'm sorry. I don't mean to put all that on you… it's just… not easy."

"I get it. And I'm sorry. I really did just lose track of time. But I know I don't always think about the fact that I'm not living on my own at the minute - I should have let you know."

The rest of the drive was quiet, but when they got home, Mum put the kettle on, and things started to feel a bit more normal.

"Mum?" Macy said, her hands wrapped around the warm mug. "In the interests of telling you things… I've been offered a new job."

"Oh?" Mum said, sitting down at the dining table with her own mug of tea.

"Back in Newcastle. It sounded like the sort of thing I'd like to do - but I'm not sure I want to move back to Newcastle."

"What would you do otherwise?"

"Stay round here, I think - although I don't know about work."

Mum smiled; "Well. I won't say anything, because I don't want to sway you, but I'm sure you know what I would like! I would say, though, that I just want you to be happy."

Macy smiled. "I know you do. And I... after everything that has happened, everything I could have lost... I want to change my story. I just need to decide how."

"Well, we'll support you, no matter what."

Macy took a deep breath. "I know you will. And to keep you totally informed - I also should mention I have a date tomorrow night."

Why was she feeling awkward about telling her mother she had a date? She was thirty for God's sake; she'd been on dates before. But there was something different about admitting in when she was living at home...

Mum's eyebrows rose. "Anyone I know?"

Macy shook her head. "He's called Sam - from the stroke group."

"That's exciting," Mum said, and Macy was relieved that she moved on. "And you're meeting up with Amelia this week?"

Yes, not sure what day though - I need to confirm. And a group of people she meets in the café... I'm not sure how it'll go, but I think it might be nice. And I was going to see if I can get a doctor's appointment, to talk about getting my driving licence back."

"I'm so proud of you," Mum said, and Macy could tell she was getting tearful.

"I'm going to run and have a shower," she said. "Sorry, again - about today."

◆ ◆ ◆

By Tuesday afternoon, she found herself nervous and rifling through her wardrobe for something to wear.

Mum came in to check up on her, but swiftly disappeared when she realised Macy's mood was not conducive to company. Macy was quickly realising that she needed new clothes. She hadn't brought everything she owned with her, of course - and she was getting fed up with the rotation. So many of her clothes were chosen for her office job, too - and were currently not very useful.

Eventually she chose a black jumper dress with black boots, and a bright blue cardigan to add a bit of colour.

"Does this look all right?" she asked Mum as she hurriedly applied some eyeliner, messing it up when her hand decided not to work properly, before quickly wiping it off and starting again.

"It looks great."

"You don't mind dropping me off?"

"Course not. Just let me know when you want picking up."

"Thanks, Mum - if it's late, I can try to get a taxi."

Mum laughed. "You know that isn't going to happen!"

"I do miss being able to call a taxi at a moment's notice," Macy said, putting her lipstick on and dabbing it with tissue in the mirror. "And having lots of takeaway options!"

"Oh, how did you survive so many years here in the wilderness," Mum said with a laugh.

Macy giggled.

"Ready?"

"Yep."

◆ ◆ ◆

It was bang on seven o'clock when she got out of the car, at the front of the little Italian restaurant Sam had suggested. It was one of very few fancy, date-worthy restaurants the town held, and Macy had eaten there a few times before - but she wasn't really focussing on the food.

She waved goodbye to Mum, and then made her

way into the restaurant, glad she had brought a coat, since it was still rather chilly once the sun had gone down.

Before she had chance to speak to the waitress who greeted her, Sam stood up and waved from a little table in the corner, with a candle and a rose in the centre.

"Hey," she said, when the waitress had shown her over.

"Hey." He was grinning, and she couldn't help but beam back. "You look lovely."

"Thank you," she said, blushing as he leant over and kissed her cheek, before sitting down. He wore a dark blue shirt and black jeans, with the top two shirt buttons undone. "You look nice too," she said, a little awkwardly.

They ordered wine, even though Macy hadn't really drunk since the stroke. She felt like she needed the liquid courage - and by how set his jaw was, she thought he did too.

They clinked glasses and drank in silence for a moment, and then both began to speak at the same time, before apologising and lapsing into silence.

"Pineapple on pizza?" Macy asked, desperate to break the awkwardness, and at least it paid off.

He laughed: "Never."

"Oh dear. I love it."

"Heathen."

She giggled. "Favourite season?"

"Winter - I love Christmas. You?"

"Summer. Bring on the sun, every time."

"You're living in the wrong country if you like sun!" he said.

She sighed dramatically. "Don't I know it."

And the questioning continued, but they didn't really need it anymore: the conversation flowed more freely than the wine, and when the food came, Macy found she was too distracted by Sam to eat much, despite how delicious it was.

"Did you tell your parents you were going on a date?" Sam asked, when they left the restaurant. He took her hand, and it felt natural for hers to be slipped inside his. They walked aimlessly, the night air fairly mild, the stars above them brighter than Macy remembered them ever being.

"Yes," she said. "Felt like a teenager again - embarrassed about telling my parents I was going out with a boy!"

"I don't want to embarrass you," Sam said.

"You don't embarrass me," she said, squeezing his

hand. "I just didn't expect to have to fill my mother in on my dates at thirty, that's all. I didn't expect any of this."

"Me neither," Sam said. "Do you want to come back to mine for coffee? It's only round the corner."

She didn't hesitate. "I'd love to."

❖ ❖ ❖

They walked back to his flat hand-in-hand, and Macy felt every nerve in her body tingling. They had said coffee - but she didn't know if that was what he meant, or what the expectations were. She wasn't even sure what she wanted.

Nerves were definitely playing a big part in her uncertainty. She knew she found him attractive, she knew she wanted to get closer to him - but since her stroke, she found she didn't really trust her body. Would it still work the same? Would his? None of this had seemed quite so complicated before the stroke.

He did put the kettle on as soon as they were back, but he also opened a bottle of wine, and Macy thought that wine might be a better choice. She didn't want to be quite so in her head as she was…

He made the coffee and brought it over, telling her to make herself at home, and she unzipped her boots, feeling bad for still wearing them in his very clean and neat flat. But without them on, she felt a little less powerful.

"I really enjoyed tonight," Sam said.

"Me too."

"I've been thinking, a lot… about what you said."

"I haven't shut up this evening," she said with a grin. "So you'll have to be a bit more specific."

"About the job, in Newcastle."

"Oh."

"I don't know if I can say this… but I would really, really like you to stay."

"Oh."

"I know I have no right to make any claims on you. And if your heart is in Newcastle, I get it. It's not that far away - we could still date, if you wanted to. But…" He paused, and glanced at the kitchen counter. "Do you want a glass of wine, as well as the coffee? Or instead?"

She nodded. "Yes please."

He grabbed the open bottle and two glasses, and somehow managed to balance them with his crutch, and made his way back to the sofa. They were silent as he opened it and poured, and she found herself both excited and nervous for what else he had to say.

He took two large gulps of the wine, and put the glass on the table, before smiling with a red-stained mouth.

"This sounds trite, but I have not felt like this about anyone… ever. Not before the stroke, and certainly not since. I really want to see where this goes - and I think that it's got a better chance if you're living near here. If that's an option. But if it's not, or I've misjudged this, or…"

Macy took a swig of her wine, before putting it next to Sam's on the coffee table, and grabbing his hand. "You've not misjudged it. And it is an option. I'll need to think…"

He nodded.

"I… I haven't felt like this either. I've been so miserable, and you've been the light in the darkness…" She felt her eyes tearing up, and blinked furiously, looking away. "Sorry. How embarrassing…"

He reached up and gently turned her head back to face him, his hand against her cheek. "It's not embarrassing."

"I'm spouting nonsense like I'm a poet, and then crying," she said, trying to roll her eyes, but finding she was too full of emotion to really put the effort into it.

His lips touched hers and she felt her heart jump wildly in her chest. Her hands moved to his waist, pulling him closer, and his grip on her face tightened. Their bodies pressed together on the sofa, and Macy felt her head going light, as lust and lack of breath warred inside her.

His lips moved to her neck, and she felt herself clutching onto him, wanting his warmth and light to be as close to her as possible. She felt truly alive, and all she wanted was more.

"Stay," he muttered into her neck. "Stay, stay… stay tonight, stay forever."

"Okay," she whispered, not even thinking about the words leaving his lips, just wanting to be closer to him, to keep feeling how she was feeling for as long as possible. Was her desire for him so much stronger than anything she had ever felt because she had been sleepwalking through life for weeks? Or was it something about Sam, and she would have felt that way whenever it had happened?

When they took a moment to catch their breath, Macy reached for her wine and polished it off. She hadn't really drunk since having the stroke, but tonight it made her feel even more alive.

"Do you… do you really want me to stay? Tonight?"

He nodded fervently. "If you want to. If not, I totally get it, I… just don't want tonight to end."

"Neither do I," Macy said. "I just… I have to text my mum," she said, and then giggled. "I know that sounds ridiculous, and it's not something I really want to do, but I think you're one of the few people who will actually understand."

He grinned, and grabbed his own glass of wine. "I totally do. They become way more protective after that brush with death… but I don't want your mum's first impression of me to be the guy who lured you into staying out late."

Macy giggled; "If I don't text her, I can't stay."

"Then text her quickly - I'll have to improve on the impression when I meet her in person."

Warmth spread through Macy at his words, as she quickly fired off a text, hoping her mum would not ask any awkward questions. It wasn't easy to admit she was staying at her date's house to her mother - but she knew it was a far better option than never ringing for a lift and making her mum terrified she had died in a ditch somewhere.

*Don't need a lift tonight - don't panic, I'm fine. Love you. X*

The response was immediate, and thankfully free of any questions. *Thanks for texting. Love you too x*

And then her phone was forgotten, as Sam's good arm wrapped around her waist, pulling her closer, until she was sat in his lap, her arms around his neck, lips pressed together, hearts racing.

# CHAPTER TEN

She woke up first the next morning, and for a few minutes had to remember where she was. The bed was different, the sheets were different, and the arms wrapped around her were certainly very different. His curtains didn't quite block out all the light, and she watched it dance around the room as she slowly turned onto her back, not wanting to wake him up.

She couldn't quite believe what had happened. All her anxiety - about her post-stroke mind, her post-stroke body, let alone his - had evaporated, and she had felt as though she could forget all of her worries for that night.

Watching him breathe deeply in and out, she smiled to herself. He was a ray of sunshine in a particularly dark few months - but now, looking back on her life, she wasn't sure it had been this light in a while. Perhaps, she thought, it wasn't just the stroke that had brought darkness. She hadn't been truly happy in a long time - not with her job, or her friends, or the direction her life was going.

"Morning." She almost jumped as Sam's voice

disturbed her thoughts. "You all right?"

She nodded, pulling the duvet tight around her, and smiled. "Yeah."

He propped himself up on one elbow, the duvet falling away from his chest. His weak arm lay on the bed, but it was barely noticeable. Macy found she didn't really think about it, except if he needed to carry things. She let her fingers rest on it, glancing back at his messy black hair and smiling lips.

"So," he said. "Are you a coffee drinker in the mornings? Or tea?"

"Coffee," she said. "And you?"

"Tea," he said, with a laugh. "And views on breakfast?"

"Very positive."

"Good to know."

Macy stretched out, and Sam reached to find pyjamas bottoms from a drawer under the bed, before putting them on and hooking his leg round his crutch to drag in towards him. It had been somewhat hastily abandoned on the floor the previous night.

"Do you need help?" Macy asked.

Sam shook his head; "I'll be back in a minute."

Macy redressed in some of her clothes, although left the tight-fitting jeans on the floor, and waited under the duvet until he returned, balancing a tray with two mugs in one hand, while holding his crutch in the other. She resisted the urge to help; he had said he didn't need it.

"Thanks," she said, mug of coffee in hand, and she leant back against the pillows, not quite so shy now she was partially dressed.

"Did I mess up?" he asked suddenly. "Was this too fast?"

She shook her head. "No, it's all good. I just… my head needs to catch up."

He grinned. "Mine too. But last night…"

"Was pretty great."

"I've only…" he said, then drank his tea. "What time do you need to leave?"

"No rush," she said. "And what were you going to say?"

"Nothing," he said. "It's not… don't worry."

She put her hand on his. "Please tell me."

"It's a really stupid thing to say when you're in bed with someone, so just forget I ever said it."

"I would like to know…"

He sighed; "Okay. But don't let this be the thing that ruins it all."

"Okay."

"I've only… slept with a woman once, since my stroke. And I worried the entire time about my deficits, and whether she was pitying me, and whether she was disgusted by me. But with you…"

"With me?"

"I forgot I'd even had a stroke."

"Me too."

They kissed, being very careful not to spill their drinks, and then Macy lay back on the pillows, Sam's arm around her.

"Now… I believe breakfast was mentioned?"

❖ ❖ ❖

They ate scrambled eggs on toast, half-dressed on the sofa, and Macy didn't think she'd giggled so much in her life. Early spring sun streamed through the windows, and Macy felt like she was living a scene from someone else's life. She didn't remember what it felt like to be this happy; this content.

Her phone beeped as Sam made them another drink, and her happy daze made her respond without thinking or stressing about the answer.

*Meeting some friends in the café at 12.30 if you want to join – no pressure. Amelia X*

*That'd be lovely – see you there. X*

She quickly fired off a text to mum, explaining that she was meeting Amelia, and asking for a lift later that afternoon, before Sam sat back down and handed her another coffee.

"Thanks."

"You're welcome – even though coffee is not usually drunk in this house before midday."

She giggled.

"So…" he said, and the word hung in the air like the dust motes that were highlighted by the sunbeams.

"So," Macy replied, unsure what exactly he was trying to address.

"Would you be open to another date?"

She grinned, blushed, and then nodded. "Definitely."

He blushed too, the colour spreading across his face beneath his now stubbled chin.

"Saturday?"

"It is the traditional date night."

"And only three days away..."

"Can you cope three whole days?" Macy said, grinning, surprised by her own boldness.

"I'll have to try," he said, a grin on his face too. "I'm working the next three days, and I'm always so tired by the end of the day..."

"Well, we can't have that," Macy said, then realised what it might sound like she was implying and blushed furiously, covering her mouth with her hands. "I mean... I didn't mean..."

Sam laughed, an unguarded sound that sent his dark hair rippling. "I know what you meant," he said with a smirk.

"I didn't... I mean –" she realised the more she said, the deeper she was going to dig herself in this hole. "You can be cruel."

"I hope you'll forgive me."

"I think I can be persuaded..." She said, and then his arms wrapped around her waist and her fingers were entwined in his hair, and their lips were pressed together, and the world around them was gradually forgotten.

◆ ◆ ◆

The smile remained on her lips as she walked to the café to meet Amelia, despite the fact that she was wearing the clothes from the night before still. No-one would know, she told herself. She had showered at Sam's, removed all traces of last night's make up from her face, and done a passable job at sorting her hair with the only comb Sam owned.

Her boots clicked on the pavement as she walked and happiness felt like it radiated through her. She was tired, yes, but she ignored that for now. She could sleep this afternoon, once she was home. There hadn't even been time to get stressed about this meeting with Amelia and her friends, for it had all fallen into place without any notice. Perhaps she was a little overdressed for a casual lunch, but she felt good.

She felt great.

She felt better than she had done in a long time - even before the stroke.

When she got to the café, the image of Sam kissing her goodbye still playing on repeat in her brain, Amelia was already there, with a group of women. They were sat at a table, perusing menus. One pushed a pram backwards and forwards; another seemed to be arguing on her phone.

"Macy! Hey! Good to see you," Amelia said, waving with enthusiasm as soon as she spied Macy. "Come over, I've saved you a seat!"

Suddenly a little self-conscious in front of all these

woman, Macy found herself glancing around to avoid their gazes, pleased the spare seat was next to Amelia.

"Hi," she said quietly.

The assembled group said their hellos and waved, and Amelia introduced everyone. Macy couldn't help but wonder if she was always so chirpy, no matter what life threw at her; she had been that way in school, and as an adult she didn't seem to have changed much.

"This is Carla," she said, indicating the red-head who had just put her phone down. "And Gwen." The blonde pushing the pram waved with her other hand. She looked a little harassed, and yet entirely lovely, all at the same time. "And then Harriet." A tall, well-dressed woman, with red lips and a powerful smile, said hello. "And then there's Ruth, but she's running late."

"As always," Carla said, and they tittered.

"Sorry, sorry," a woman - presumably Ruth - said, rushing in, a little breathless, carrying several bags. Her curls were piled on top of her head in a bun, and the glasses on the edge of her nose looked in danger of falling off.

"It's fine," Amelia said, "You're not that late! This is Macy - we went to school together, and she's back in the area for a bit."

Once they'd sat down, and the attention had moved off her, Macy began to relax a little. They all seemed kind, but it was a while since she had spent so much time with other people, and she was worried it showed. Her head started to pound - from the stress? The late night? Another stroke? She took several deep breaths to calm herself. It wasn't another stroke; headaches were perfectly normal. She hadn't got much sleep the night before - that was all.

"You grew up here then?" Carla asked, as Macy tried to discreetly take some painkillers that were now had a permanent place in her handbag.

Macy nodded. "Yeah - moved to Newcastle at eighteen though."

"I can imagine it's quiet round here for a teenager!"

Macy laughed; "It definitely is. One nightclub and barely a bus to be seen!"

"I only moved here a year ago - my husband's work moved him, so here we are."

"Do you like it?" Macy asked, ordering a salad from the waitress who was circling the table. It wasn't that long since she'd had breakfast, but she didn't want to be rude and eat nothing when the others were having lunch.

"It's pretty," she said. "But not a lot going on…"

"You can get the train to Edinburgh, or Newcastle, fairly easily - if you want city life," she said.

"I never seem to get round to it, but I should. What made you want to move back?"

"I…" Macy said, and paused. Because this still wasn't permanent, was it - and she needed to make a lot of decisions about that very fact. Words said in the heat of passion to Sam were one thing; decisions in the cold light of day were another. "I've not been well. I'm living with my parents for a bit."

"Sorry to hear that," Carla said, pouring her lemonade into the glass that had been brought.

Macy attempted to do the same, but she lost her grip on the can, and it crashed to the table, sending its contents everywhere. The ladies jumped up to avoid it spilling onto their clothes, and Macy was mortified.

"Sorry, sorry, sorry," she said over and over, as the waitress rushed over with a cloth and a mop. "I'm so clumsy…" She knew it was probably thanks to the stroke, but found she didn't want to announce it to a group of people she had only just met. She didn't want it to be the only thing they associated her with.

"It's fine, it's fine," Amanda said breezily, and soon enough they were all sat down again, the incident almost forgotten.

The chatter swelled around Macy, and she was amazed to notice that well over an hour had passed by the time the waitress came to get their money. She had learnt that Gwen was divorced; Harriet seemed to have a very well-paying career, although she wasn't quite sure in what field; and Ruth was a hairdresser. She found that, in spite of the headache and exhaustion that she was battling, she was glad she had come - and when Amelia suggested she join them the following week, she agreed with unexpected enthusiasm.

Still, she knew she was reaching her body's limit, and when Mum turned up only fifteen minutes after she had text her, she was beyond grateful.

"You look done in," Mum said, when Macy got in the car and let out a loud sigh.

"I have socialised more today that I have in… well, a very long time!"

"Was it good?"

"Yeah… it was actually."

"And the date?"

She grinned, then blushed, and was very glad her mother could not read her thoughts. "Yeah, that was good too. We're going out again Saturday."

"Sounds like everything's working out," Mum said.

"It does, doesn't it?" Macy said with a smile. "But for now... I need sleep."

❖ ❖ ❖

On Friday, Macy had a neurologist appointment at the hospital, and decided to go alone. Her mother wasn't keen, but Macy felt as though this bit of independence was something she really needed; it was time to see what she could do, standing on her own two feet.

There were so many decisions to be made. About where she would live; where she would work; what her life was going to look like now. But she wasn't sure how she was meant to make any of the decisions while still living at home, and barely leaving the house alone. So she got her mum to drop her into town, and took the train by herself back to Newcastle, and then walked to the hospital.

There were far too many bad memories at the hospital, but she hoped that today's appointment might be a good memory. Might be a start of moving her life forwards.

When she was called in, the neurologist was smiling, and Macy wondered whether that was a good sign, or just how she always acted.

"Miss Maxwell. How are you getting on?"

Macy shrugged. What a complicated question. "Improving, I think. Still struggling with dropping things, and being exhausted..."

"Yes, the after-effects of a stroke can last a long time I'm afraid. But you're showing good progress. Now, the reason I brought you here – I believe we found the cause of your stroke."

"Really?"

The neurologist nodded. "The team had a look at your scans, and have found a tear in your artery. A clot must've broken loose, and blocked the blood flow to your brain."

"How does that happen? The tear, I mean?"

"It's hard to say. You haven't been a car accident, had you? Or had your hair washed at a hairdresser's sink? Or been painting ceilings... Or anything like that?"

Macy shook her head. "No, nothing that I can think of. I think my neck might have ached for a few days beforehand, but nothing that I can put my finger on..."

The neurologist nodded. "We'll probably never be certain, I'm afraid. Possibly some people are genetically more prone to it happening, but we just don't know. There's no reason to suspect it will happen again though, and once it's healed, and the risk is significantly reduced, you can come off all medication."

"Wow," Macy said, her mind reeling.

"I thought you might feel a bit better, knowing why you had the stroke."

Macy nodded, and fiddled with the strap on a handbag. "Yes, I think I do, it's just... A lot of new information."

They worked through a few neurological tests, and the doctor was happy to sign off on Macy driving again, considering everything. Scans were booked in, and a timeline of stopping medication discussed. When Macy left, she felt like her mind was a little scrambled, and yet surely this appointment had been everything she had wanted? An explanation, a little lowered anxiety perhaps, the date for finishing this medication that made her feel like she was a hundred years old.

She decided to check in at her flat, since it had been so long since she had been there. So many decisions to be made... If she was going to come back and work in the city, she would need the flat – but if she wasn't, if she was going to stay in Northumberland, if she was going to stay with Sam, then it was just eating up her finances.

The key fit smoothly in the lock, although opening it felt like a door to another life. All other things were still there, and yet her life had moved on.

She sat on the sofa for a moment, her body tired and protesting at the busy day it'd had. It felt odd to be alone, to be in such quiet, and she toyed with the idea of pulling her phone out and ringing her mother, to tell her what neurologist had said. But she would see her that evening; she was meant to be standing on her own two feet. Before all this, she had been perfectly used to being alone for long periods of time...

As she stood to fetch a glass of water she felt dizzy, and for the first time in a while, the overwhelming anxiety of something terrible about to happen hit her. Was it being in this flat, where something terrible had happened? Or had she just overdone it? She didn't know, but she wished someone was here with her, wished someone would talk her down from the ledge of panic she found herself on.

Eventually she forced herself to lock back up, and walk the short distance to the train station. Her heart was racing, and it was taking everything within her not to burst into tears - although she wasn't entirely sure why.

Once she sat herself down on the train, and fished a small bottle of water from the bottom of her handbag, she tried to take deep breaths. She would be home soon - back in Northumberland, where there were people to keep an eye on her. She would be all right; she was not having another stroke.

She'd just overdone it, and now anxiety was taking hold. That had to be it. She hadn't even walked that far or that fast.

"Tickets please," the conductor said, and she showed him her digital ticket, before resting her head on the seat in front and focussing on the in and out of her breathing, the floor beneath her feet, and the sounds of the tannoy announcements in the station.

*Can you pick me up from the station in an hour? Not feeling well x* She hit send on the message to her mother, knowing that at least she could be at home and in bed within a couple of hours, and then everything would feel better.

It would all be okay.

There were so many decisions to make, but first of all, she just needed to get home.

# CHAPTER ELEVEN

*Can we take a rain check on tonight? Not feeling great, sorry.* Macy text from her darkened bedroom on Saturday morning. She debated putting a kiss on the end - she *had* slept with the guy, after all - but didn't in the end. She was gutted to be postponing their second date, but since coming back from Newcastle, she had been having the most horrendous migraine - bad enough that she was wondering if a trip to A and E was warranted. She had spent the night waking and then taking more painkillers and attempting to go back to sleep - and the only thing stopping her parents from dragging her to the hospital was that she didn't have the vomiting or the vertigo like she had done before.

Mum knocked quietly and then came in with a cup of a tea and a cold flannel, and Macy wriggled to sit herself up against the pillows. She hated spending the day in bed, but she felt too ill to get up and do anything.

"How are you doing?" Mum asked, putting the cold cloth on Macy's forehead.

"Not great," Macy said, trying to hold back tears.

"Oh love."

"I just… I thought I was ready. And now I'm bed-bound because I was out for the day."

"It's not been that long, Macy. You had a stroke! You can't expect to just bounce back."

"I know. But it's been weeks. And I'm only thirty… I don't want to spend my life like this."

"You won't. It will get better."

"I'm scared…"

"We can ring the doctor."

"Let's give it another hour," Macy said. "I really don't want to spend all afternoon in A and E."

"You never told me how Newcastle was," Mum said.

"Oh… they found the cause of my stroke. Tear to the artery, like they thought."

"Well, that's something," Mum said. "At least that shouldn't mean you need to worry about it happening again, right?"

"Yeah. And they think I can come off the meds,

once it's healed."

Mum squeezed Macy's arm. "Things are looking up already."

"I felt so alone," Macy said, sipping her tea and avoiding Mum's piercing gaze. "In Newcastle."

"Yesterday?"

"Yesterday… and before. But yesterday I felt ill, and scared, and there was no-one to turn to…"

"You don't have to go back," Mum said.

"I don't think I want to."

"You can stay with us as long as you like."

Macy smiled. "I know that, and I really appreciate it… but I think I need to look for somewhere of my own. But close by…"

"We'll help. You know how much your father loves perusing estate agents' windows."

Macy laughed, but found the motion hurt her head. "I don't want to be on my own any more."

"You don't have to be."

❖ ❖ ❖

By the time the allotted hour was up, Macy was finally sleeping deeply, and when she woke up that evening, she felt well enough to get up and eat some plain pasta. A trip to hospital seemed to have been avoided, thank goodness.

*Of course we can. You ok? X*

She hadn't felt up to reading her messages earlier in the day, and felt guilty, for it was almost time for the date that she had ended up cancelling. She smiled, though, when she saw the kiss at the end of the message. Perhaps she had been over-thinking things.

*Terrible migraine. Think I've overdone it lately. I'm sorry. X*

*As long as you're ok. We can reschedule! X*

*Tuesday? X*

*Perfect. Hope you feel better x*

She spent the evening in front of the television with her parents, but found she wasn't really watching. Her mind was in overdrive.

She didn't want to live in the city, isolated from her family.

She didn't want to live an hour away from Sam.

So the job in Newcastle was out of the question - and the flat could be let go of. They were decisions, at least, that she didn't need to obsess over any more.

For now, she made a mental list of what she needed to do: Find a job. Find a flat. Empty her old flat. Talk to Sam.

Talk to Sam.

She didn't want to scare him, and it wasn't as if her decision to stay was entirely based on him, but he definitely had an impact. She was happier with him than she had been in… well, a very long time. And he understood her better than anyone; understood the way this stroke had changed her, on the inside. Even though he hadn't known her before.

Nibbling on a rich tea biscuit, she tried to push away the anxiety she felt over her health. This migraine hadn't helped matters: was she destined to feel so ill every time she pushed herself a little? When would she stop panicking that every twinge was another stroke?

She needed to pace herself a bit more, that's what her father said - but she was only thirty. She didn't want to pace herself.

Still. She was doing so, even if it was subconsciously. She would probably leave stroke group on Monday, so as not to push herself, and had intentionally rescheduled the date for Tuesday. That way, there wasn't too much going on in one day - and, assuming she stayed the night Tuesday, she would then spend Wednesday looking for flats and jobs that she felt capable of doing, and meeting Amelia for lunch.

The doctor had said she could drive, too: something else to start doing. Maybe she could go out with dad to start with, just until she got her confidence back. He was far calmer than mum in the passenger seat: a memorable driving lesson with mum where Macy had thought she said 'go', but she had in fact said 'whoa', had ended any such excursions.

So many things to do - but hopefully that meant living life again properly, rather than just making it through each day.

❖ ❖ ❖

She was more excited than nervous when their second date finally rolled around, and although she was still tired, she was relieved that the migraine had gone away without the need for major medical intervention.

Unfortunately, feeling so ill on the way back from Newcastle had ruined her plan of bringing some more of her clothes back with her, so once more she found herself rummaging through a small amount of garments to put together an outfit for the date. Ending up with the same black skinny jeans, but this time with a sparkly top and flat shoes, she asked Mum to give her a lift, deciding to leave driving again for the first time in weeks to when she wasn't in a hurry, or anxious.

Sam had offered to cook, and so Macy arrived at his flat, with a bottle of wine in one hand, and her handbag in the other. She didn't want to look like she was expecting to stay - but she had packed a few essentials in there, just in case it ended up happening. She certainly wasn't averse to the idea, and had awkwardly confirmed with Mum when she had been dropped off that she might not be home that night.

Sam opened the door with a grin on his face, wearing a dark blue shirt that was open at the neck, and dark blue trousers to match.

"Hey," he said, stepping out the way to let her in. "It's good to see you." He leant in to kiss her on the cheek, and she smelled his aftershave and felt a tingle go through her at his proximity.

"You too," she said. "Sorry about the other night."

"It's fine," he said, as they moved into the living room. "Are you feeling better though? Because I don't want you to push yourself."

"Much better," she said, putting the wine down on the counter top. "It smells delicious - do you need any help?"

"It's all in hand," he said, handing her two glasses. "I won't say no to a glass of that wine, though."

She poured the red wine carefully into two glasses, before taking a large sip of hers.

They chatted about his work, and the improving weather, before getting on to the trigger for her migraine - her trip to Newcastle.

"So," Sam said, stirring something that sizzled away on the hob. "What did the neurologist have to say?"

"They found a tear," she said. "In my artery, in my neck. Once it's healed, I should be able to come off the medication."

"That's brilliant!" he said, with a grin. "Isn't it?"

Macy found she struggled to return his smile. "Yeah… It is. I just… I still feel so ill. And I get overwhelmed so easily, and it takes so little for everything to get thrown off…" Tears pricked her eyes. "Sorry," she said, wiping at them furiously. "I didn't come over here to get upset!"

He put down the wooden spoon and wiped his hands on a tea towel, then came and wrapped his arms around her. She leant into his solid chest, and took a few deep breaths. "Sorry."

"You don't need to apologise. And if you want to come here and cry, or shout, or vent - I'm fine with all that. I mean, I'd rather you weren't sad. But if you are… you don't need to hide it from me."

Macy sniffed. "It's just been a lot. The last few days. My head feels like it's whirling…"

"As long as it's not vertigo," Sam said, and they both laughed at the dark humour.

"What are you cooking for me, then?" Macy asked as he returned to the stove.

"Risotto," he said. "Are you hungry?"

"Starving," she said.

"Good."

"I've been thinking…"

"Sounds ominous."

"It's not," Macy said, taking another sip of wine for courage. "Big, but not ominous."

He paused in whatever it was he was doing on the stove top. "Okay…"

"I don't want to move back to Newcastle."

He grinned. "You made it sound like it was something bad!"

"I didn't say bad - just big."

"I don't want you to move back to Newcastle."

"You don't?" Her heart felt like a tennis ball, jumping around inside her chest. Yes he had asked her to stay, that first night - but she had thought they were merely words spoken in passion.

"I think you already knew I didn't," he murmured. "But you don't want to go back?"

"I don't want to be isolated any more," she said. "From my family… my friends… or you. So I'm going to give up my flat there."

"And stay with your parents?"

"For now - but I'm going to look for a flat in town, so I can get around easily, and have some independence."

"Sounds perfect."

"Although… they've said I can drive, too."

"Excellent," Sam said, with another wide beam. "I always need a chauffeur."

Macy giggled.

"But seriously, that's great - and I see what you mean, big week. No wonder you set off a migraine."

"You don't mind me staying then?"

"Why would I mind?"

Macy swallowed, and gulped some more wine, although she was well aware that it was going to her head, especially considering she was drinking it on an empty stomach.

"I dunno. I thought it might seem a bit… like commitment."

"I don't mind commitment," he said, and the air around them seem to shimmer with unspoken words for a moment, before settling back down.

"Good."

"So you've got a lot to sort then."

Macy nodded. "New flat, new job, emptying my old flat…"

"I know I'm a bit useless," he said, "With the lifting, and the driving, but I'll help in any way I can."

Macy couldn't resist moving behind him, and wrapping her arms round his waist. "You're not useless," she said, pressing a kiss to the back of his neck carefully, so as not to make him jump and hurt himself with the hot contents of the pan. "You are far from useless."

He pushed the pan off the heat, and turned so they were facing each other, their lips close enough that it was no effort for them to meet. Wrapped in each other's arms, they stumbled to the sofa, Sam not bothering to grab his crutch, and using Macy for support instead.

By the time they got to eat the risotto, it was a little dry, but they both felt it was a sacrifice they were happy to make.

❖ ❖ ❖

In the end, her leaving wasn't really discussed, and Macy woke up next to Sam on Wednesday morning, feeling all together more positive about life. He was happy she was staying; now she just needed to work on the logistics.

She was meeting Amelia and the others for lunch, but Sam had a job to get to, and although he offered for her to spend the morning in his flat, it didn't hold the same appeal without him.

"I've got plenty to get on with," she said, kissing him with minty-fresh breath, thanks to the toothbrush she had thrown into her handbag just in case.

"Don't overdo it!"

"I'll try not to."

"When am I seeing you next?" he asked, as they stood outside his front door, poised to start their days separately.

"Stroke group…" Macy suggested.

"And outside of that?"

She grinned. "When do you want to see me?"

"I don't want to scare you off."

"I'm not going anywhere," she said.

"Saturday night, then? We could do the cinema if you like."

"I would offer to cook for you," Macy said. "But I'm rubbish in the kitchen."

"I doubt you're rubbish at anything," Sam said. "But why don't we get a takeaway?"

"Then let's watch a film at yours. Better than having to be silent in a cinema."

"Deal," Sam said, and with one more kiss, he had disappeared round the corner, and Macy prepared to attack her list of jobs.

Her first stop was the art shop that she had been to the morning after her first date with Sam. Something had stuck in the back of her mind, and she needed to check it out before the rest of her searching.

The little bell above the door dinged as she entered, and the shopkeeper turned to her with a smile. No-one else was in there, and the lady said hello before turning back to the paperwork she was filling in.

Macy ignored the temptation to peruse the art supplies, and instead went to the noticeboard on the wall. The signs all seemed to be the same as when she had been the previous week - and she was glad she had returned.

*Art lessons by local teacher. All abilities. Contact 07417562386*

*Help wanted in busy art shop. Apply within.*

*Missing cat - black and white, with white patch over eye. Call 07563282956 if sighted.*

*Designer required for local business. Email josie.white@net.com for more information.*

She read back through them, and jotted down the email for the designer job. It was a lead, at least. Then she turned to the woman behind the desk, took a deep breath, and interrupted her once more.

"Hello. Is the advert on the board for this art shop?"

The lady looked at her over tortoiseshell glasses, perched on the end of her nose. "Yes, it is," she said. "Are you interested?"

Macy nodded. "I'd love some more information."

Half an hour later, after bonding over a preferred brand of paint, they had set up a trial shift for Macy on Friday. She was a little nervous about how she would cope with a long day, but she knew she needed to start bringing some money again - and whilst this certainly wouldn't pay as well as her old job, she thought she might enjoy it a whole lot more.

She was early at the cafe for lunch, but Amelia was already there, looking tired.

"Amelia," she called, as she made her way to the large table. Once she was closer, she asked, "Are you okay?"

"Late night," she said, seemingly not wanting to discuss it further. "How are you?"

"Okay," Macy said, with a shrug. Things certainly weren't amazing, health-wise - but they were looking up in every other aspect. "I think I might have found a new job."

"Oh?"

"Yeah… only a few shifts, in the art shop down the road."

Amelia smiled; "You're staying then?"

She nodded. "I need to find somewhere to live, but yeah… this is where I want to be."

The rest of the group came in then, chattering noisily, and Macy was warmed to see how quickly they accepted her as one of them.

Gwen - the slightly harassed looking blonde pushing a pram - took the seat next to Macy, and grinned. She rocked the pram backwards and forwards, and Macy wondered what would happen if she stopped.

"Nice to see you again!"

"And you."

"Looks like Macy's sticking around for a while," Amelia said.

"Excellent!" Gwen said.

"That's good news!"

"Didn't your brother have somewhere he was trying to rent out, Ruth?" someone asked, and Macy turned in the direction of Ruth, who was on time today.

"I'm looking for somewhere, if he is!"

The hour passed by in a haze of noise and chaos and friendship, and although it exhausted Macy, she left with a possible lead on a flat to rent, and a smile on her face.

She needed time to recover from the socialising - but she also needed to be surrounded by people, she had realised. And all the women seemed like they could become good friends - if she put in the time and effort.

But now it was time for a rest, she thought, as she text Mum and asked for a lift. A nap, a good home-cooked dinner, and then maybe some driving practice, before she let herself loose on the big wide world again.

She was exhausted; but things were looking up.

# CHAPTER TWELVE

## *Epilogue*

Macy stood on the bridge, looking out over the sparkling river, and smiled. Summer was in full swing, and even if it never got that hot this far north, it still meant ice creams and days at the beach and floaty summer dresses.

The last six months had brought so many things she would not have expected. The stroke, for one, of course; that was the thing she would never have predicted, not in a million years. The joy she found in moving home; the friends she had met or rediscovered; the job that she didn't dread going in to.

And then there was Sam.

Sam… who brought light and warmth every day of the week, no matter the season. Sam, who had faced the troubles Macy had, and come out positive and wise. Sam, who she spent at least three nights of the week with, every week.

Life had its challenges: she still forgot her route if she drove somewhere she didn't know well, and dropping things had become rather regular. If she stayed up too late, she knew about it the next day, and the headaches were something she hoped would disappear before too long.

But she was alive, and standing on a glorious bridge, with the sun shining down on her.

And today, that felt like enough.

She turned at the sound of a familiar noise, and grinned at the sight of Sam walking towards her, in a t-shirt, jeans, and aviator sunglasses.

"Can I carry them off, do you think?" he asked.

"You still look hot," she said, pressing a kiss to his lips.

"As long as you think so!"

"Where are you off to?"

"Came to see if you were stood up here again."

"I love it."

"You should paint a picture if you love it so much."

They both laughed; an in-joke, for they both knew she had spent countless hours trying to recreate the scene before them.

"Haven't you got work?"

"Finished early," he said.

"You can come with me, if you like, to the stroke café."

"Go on then."

They walked together through the bustling streets, to the project that Macy had started volunteering at a few months before. Well, she'd had the idea, and suggested it to Lexi, and it had become a fairly regular event: an hour at a café for stroke survivors, with a talk by someone and then some time for coffee, cake, and chat. It was on top of the regular stroke group, but a bit more structured. They'd had a driving instructor first - that one had been Macy's idea, as she tried to get her confidence in driving back. Then there was a wheelchair provider, and a masseuse, and even someone who created a brain training app. Macy did most of the research on the speakers, and Lexi did the organisation - but the events were always well-attended.

"I don't want to distract you from your work," he said, as they approached the café - the same one that Macy met her friends in every week.

Macy giggled. "You mean distract all the other people, right? We all know you're their favourite."

"Hey! I knew most of these people before you were on the scene."

"And now they're jealous of me, because I get you all the time."

He smiled his brilliant smile. "They can be jealous if they like - but it won't change that."

"Good," Macy said, squeezing his hand and opening the cafe door.

The hour went by in a whirlwind, as it always seemed to, and as Macy and Sam left hand-in-hand, the sunshine still streaming down, Macy felt like things had somehow fallen into place.

"Macy!" a voice on the other side of the pavement called, and Macy shaded her eyes to see Amelia, who checked for cars before skipping over to them - actually skipping. Macy was still surprised by her positivity all the time.

"Hey, Amelia," Macy said.

"You're both still coming to dinner on Wednesday, right?"

Sam nodded; "We'll be there!"

"Excellent. And see you at the cafe tomorrow?"

"I'll be there," Macy said. It had become a regular event, now, and she realised how much she had missed out on before, not having friends she saw regularly. With her work at the art shop, designing for an up-and-coming ice cream company on the side, the stroke cafe, stroke group, Sam, her friends, and her parents, she rarely had a moment to herself anymore; and she loved it.

They waved goodbye and carried on up the street, in the direction of Macy's work and Sam's flat. It was rather handy the two were so close; they spent most weeknights at Sam's, only really venturing to Macy's on weekends when she didn't need to be up and in work so early.

"See you later?" Sam said, as they reached the fork that would separate them.

"Of course," she said, a grin on her lips. "You're cooking!"

"As usual."

"I'll bring dessert," Macy said, pressing a kiss to his lips, before letting go of his hand to head in the other direction.

"Love you," Sam said, and Macy took two steps before realising what he had said.

She wheeled round, and he looked as though he were frozen to the spot.

"Sorry, I, that just, I-"

Macy walked back towards him. "We haven't said that," she said, her voice a little shaky.

"I know. I just… sorry, this is a terrible time to say it, I just, I say it in my head, and it just came out, and-" His face was tinged red, and Macy reached forward to take his hand again, her heart hammering in her chest.

"You say it in your head?"

He swallowed, and then his eyes met hers. "I say it in my head."

"You can say it out loud."

"I love you."

"I love you too."

Not minding who was on the street, Sam's strong arm snaked around her waist, pulling her tight, and hers ended up in his hair, as their lips crashed together in an outpouring of a love that they had both not been voicing. Now it was out in the open, in the glorious sunshine, and it felt like the world was full of so many possibilities.

"I have to get back to work," Macy whispered, when they tore themselves apart.

"Okay. I love you."

"I love you."

# AFTERWORD

I am exceptionally proud of this book, but it was not the easiest to write. Much like Macy, I had a stroke at the age of twenty-nine (although a little further away from my 30th birthday than hers!) and my whole life was suddenly very different than it always had been. Recovering from something that everyone associates with older people, plus having a toddler to take care of, has been one of the biggest challenges of my life.

And just like Macy, there has been a lot of emotions involved in that recovery. But ultimately I am very grateful to still be here, and that I am still able to write the books I love to write so much.

Unlike Macy, I was already very happily married before my stroke - but I do love to write a love story!

Thank you for taking the time to read this book. I appreciate it more than I can say.
Rebecca x

P.S You can sign up for my newsletter here: tiny.cc/paulinyi for updates, release, sales, and pictures of my family and dog!

Book Two in the Thirties Club series will be coming later this year: mybook.to/30sclub2

# THE THIRTIES CLUB

Follow these inspirational women as they turn thirty and find their lives and loves turned upside down.

## At The Stroke Of Thirty

Just about to turn thirty, Macy Maxwell is loving her life. A busy social life, interesting work and a decent salary, she thinks she's got it all figured out. And so what if she thought she'd be married with kids by the time she turned thirty? Life is easy and fun.

And then, the night before her thirtieth birthday, everything changes. A near-fatal stroke leaves Macy re-evaluating everything in her life, as she tries to heal and get back the woman she was before.

Will moving back to rural Northumberland, a stroke support group and a handsome shoulder to cry on help her to find the Macy was - or help her become the Macy she wants to be?

Fans of Sophie Kinsella and JoJo Moyes will love this heart-warming tale of rebuilding a life, finding love and the twists and turns in life's journey.

'At the Stroke of Thirty' is book one in 'The Thirties Club' series, but can be read as a standalone novel.

## Life Begins At Thirty

Life, love, and heartbreak.

Amelia had always been thought of as unusually happy - until grief robber her of all her joy.

Can she find a reason to love life again?

Book Two in The Thirties Club series, coming soon!

# BOOKS BY THIS AUTHOR

**The Worst Christmas Ever?**

**Lawyers And Lattes**

**Feeling The Fireworks**

**The Best Christmas Ever**

**Trouble In Tartan**

**Summer Of Sunshine**

**The Love Of A Lord**

**Can't Let My Heart Fall**

**Misrule My Heart**

**Saving Grace's Heart**

**Learning To Love Once More**

**An Innocent Heart**

**Let Love Grow**

Printed in Great Britain
by Amazon